序 言

　　自「全民英語能力分級檢定測驗」實施以來，參加考試的人數逐年增加，預計在未來，所有國小、國中學生，以及一般社會人士，如計程車駕駛、百貨業、餐飲業、旅遊業或觀光景點服務人員、維修技術人員、一般行政助理等，均須通過「初級英語能力檢定測驗」，以作爲畢業、就業、升遷時之英語能力證明，已是必然趨勢，此項測驗的重要性，由此可見。

　　「初級英檢模擬試題④」完全仿照「初級英語能力檢定測驗」初試的題型，書中包括「聽力測驗」以及「閱讀能力測驗」，希望能幫助讀者輕鬆通過初級檢定的初試測驗。

　　全書共收錄了四回的模擬試題，每個題目均附有詳細的中文翻譯、單字註解或文法解說，好讓讀者不只能藉由練習來熟悉考題模式，更能藉由每回試題的詳解，加強自己的英文實力。

　　本書的完成，是「學習出版公司」團隊的力量。全書由蔡惠婷小姐擔任總指揮，感謝美籍老師 Laura E. Stewart，以及謝靜芳老師、林工富老師、李書琳老師、及楊玉潔老師熱心校訂，白雪嬌小姐設計封面，黃淑貞小姐設計版面及編排，陳又嘉小姐繪製插圖。

　　本書雖經審慎校對，但恐疏漏之處在所難免，盼各界先進不吝批評指正。

編者 謹識

全民英語能力分級檢定測驗
初級測驗①

一、聽力測驗

　　本測驗分三部份，全爲三選一之選擇題，每部份各 10 題，共 30
題，作答時間約 20 分鐘。

第一部份：看圖辨義

　　　　本部份共 10 題，試題冊上每題有一個圖片，請聽錄音機
　　　　播出一個相關的問題，與 A、B、C 三個英語敘述後，選
　　　　一個與所看到圖片最相符的答案，並在答案紙上相對的圓
　　　　圈內塗黑作答。每題播出一遍，問題及選項均不印在試題
　　　　冊上。

例：（看）

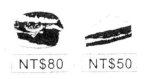

NT$80　　NT$50

（聽）

Look at the picture.   How
much is the hamburger?

　　A. It's eighty dollars.
　　B. It's fifty-five dollars.
　　C. It's eighteen dollars.

正確答案爲 A

A. Questions 1-2

B. Question 3

C. Question 4

D. Question 5

請翻頁 ⫸

E. Question 6

F. Question 7

G. Question 8

H. Question 9

I. Question 10

5-Day Weather Forecast

Monday	Tuesday	Wednesday	Thursday	Friday

請 翻 頁 ◀ ⟹

第二部份：問答

　　　本部份共 10 題，每題錄音機會播出一個問句或直述句，
　　　每題播出一次，聽後請從試題冊上 A、B、C 三個選項中，
　　　選出一個最適合的回答或回應，並在答案紙上塗黑作答。

　　例：

　　（聽）　Good morning, Kevin.　How are you?

　　（看）　A.　I'm fine, thank you.
　　　　　　B.　I'm in the living room.
　　　　　　C.　My name is Kevin.

　　　　正確答案為 A

11. A. Yes, it's your turn.
　　B. Yes, it's 12:00 a.m.
　　C. No, it's only eleven
　　　　a.m.

12. A. It must be from the
　　　　bakery.
　　B. I made it myself.
　　C. It came from Tainan
　　　　last night.

13. A. They're on the
　　　　second shelf.
　　B. Yes, but not very well.
　　C. No, I couldn't eat
　　　　another bowl.

14. A. Yes, one of them is.
　　B. The one on the left.
　　C. I have a very large
　　　　family.

15. A. Are you sure that will be enough for one person?
    B. But we only need ten.
    C. The chocolate ones are better.

16. A. No, I always take a taxi.
    B. Yes, we're nearly there.
    C. Yes, at six a.m.

17. A. No, I haven't heard from him.
    B. Of course. He's famous.
    C. I'm sorry. He's not here now.

18. A. Yes, I think it's a great price.
    B. I put it in the closet.
    C. No, I'm afraid it's beyond repair.

19. A. Either one will do.
    B. No, I'm not cold.
    C. Yes, I would.

20. A. Of course you may. Here you are.
    B. No, it's right here.
    C. Sorry. I'll close it.

請 翻 頁 ⟹

第三部份： 簡短對話

本部份共 10 題，每題錄音機會播出一段對話及一個相關的問題，每題播出兩次，聽後請從試題冊上 A、B、C 三個選項中，選出一個最適合的回答，並在答案紙上塗黑作答。

例：

(聽) (Woman) Good afternoon, …Mr. Davis?

(Man) Yes. I have an appointment with Dr. Sanders at two o'clock. My son Tommy has a fever.

(Woman) Oh, that's too bad. Well, please have a seat, Mr. Davis. Dr. Sanders will be right with you.

Question: Where did this conversation take place?

(看) A. In a post office.

B. In a restaurant.

C. In a doctor's office.

正確答案為 C

21. A. She cannot play an
    instrument well.
    B. She has never played
    the piano.
    C. She can play only the
    piano well.

22. A. She is afraid of the man.
    B. She will give Jill the
    message.
    C. She is afraid that Jill
    will come home soon.

23. A. She thinks he is not a
    good friend.
    B. He is hard to get along
    with.
    C. She thinks he might be
    lazy.

24. A. He is not yet
    seven.
    B. He is taller than
    he was last year.
    C. He is the tallest in
    his family.

25. A. He is very strong.
    B. He is very kind.
    C. He is very brave.

26. A. To the post office.
    B. To a store.
    C. To the shopping
    mall.

請 翻 頁 ⟹

27. A. She erased one of
    the numbers.
  B. She forgot to write
    one of the numbers.
  C. She could not
    remember the
    telephone number.

28. A. He was not tall
    enough.
  B. He was looking on
    the wrong shelf.
  C. The closet was too
    dark.

29. A. That the man ask
    God for help.
  B. That the man
    prepare for the test
    right away.
  C. That the man start
    studying sooner next
    time.

30. A. He went to Canada.
  B. He went during the
    winter.
  C. His parents made
    him go.

二、閱讀能力測驗

本測驗分三部份，全為四選一之選擇題，共 35 題，作答時間 35 分鐘。

第一部份： 詞彙和結構

本部份共15題，每題含一個空格。請就試題冊上 A、B、C、D 四個選項中選出最適合題意的字或詞，標示在答案紙上。

1. I was tired, so I _____ down on the sofa and slept.
   A. lay
   B. laid
   C. lain
   D. lied

2. "Ian, you never learned to drive, _____?"
   A. did you
   B. doesn't you
   C. didn't you
   D. aren't you

3. I want to learn painting _____ my vacation in Taipei.
   A. while
   B. until
   C. during
   D. for

請 翻 頁 ▌▌⟹

4. The notice was written _____ a crayon.

   A. from

   B. in

   C. of

   D. with

5. Your son will be _____ Mozart in the future.

   A. one

   B. the

   C. a

   D. same

6. I have two English dictionaries; one is big and _____ is small.

   A. the other

   B. the one

   C. another

   D. either

7. The lady _____ Iris lives with is my sister.

   A. who

   B. whose

   C. whom

   D. that

8. If I had taken your advice then, I _____ the work now.
   A. finished
   B. have finished
   C. would have finished
   D. had finished

9. I will wait in the rain until Sara _____ the door.
   A. opened
   B. opens
   C. had opened
   D. will open

10. Stop _____ that video game! Have you finished your homework?
    A. to play
    B. to playing
    C. played
    D. playing

11. This closet was _____ a teak wood, so it's quite expensive.
    A. made from
    B. made on
    C. made in
    D. made of

請 翻 頁 ▐▊⟹

12. I don't want _____ pepper in my soup. Just a little, please.
    A. any
    B. some
    C. many
    D. much

13. She _____ a beautiful girl, but she is an old lady now.
    A. is used to be
    B. was used to be
    C. used to being
    D. used to be

14. My bicycle was stolen, so I have to go home _____ foot.
    A. from
    B. with
    C. on
    D. in

15. Amy will leave _____ Paris next week. There will be big sales in Paris then.
    A. for
    B. by
    C. in
    D. from

第二部份：段落填空

本部份共 10 題，包括二個段落，每個段落各含 5 個空格。請就試題冊上 A、B、C、D 四個選項中選出最適合題意的字或詞，標示在答案紙上。

Questions 16-20

Some people try ____(16)____ to have better things than other people, so they ____(17)____ money from friendly banks. They can buy anything they want, but the money they spend is not ____(18)____. This materialistic（物質的）world has ____(19)____ our young generation very much. Some young people use credit cards to buy things they want. They don't care ____(20)____ they have enough money to pay back the banks.

16. A. hardly
    B. hard
    C. often
    D. sincerely

17. A. borrow
    B. lend
    C. bring
    D. spend

18. A. theirs
    B. their's
    C. their
    D. them

19. A. improved
    B. influenced
    C. offered
    D. puzzled

20. A. that
    B. about
    C. for
    D. if

請翻頁 ⬛⟹

Questions 21-25

I'm fond of ___(21)___ emails to people from other

countries. My favorite online friend lives in Italy. I ___(22)___

a letter to him two weeks ago. I haven't received an answer to

that letter ___(23)___. Maybe my English is ___(24)___ poor that

he didn't understand what I ___(25)___.

21. A. write
    B. to write
    C. writing
    D. wrote

22. A. sent
    B. send
    C. have sent
    D. was sending

23. A. still
    B. really
    C. already
    D. yet

24. A. very
    B. so
    C. much
    D. too

25. A. write
    B. have written
    C. writing
    D. wrote

第三部份： 閱讀理解

本部份共 10 題，包括數段短文，每段短文後有 1～3 個相
關問題，請就試題冊上 A、B、C、D 四個選項中選出最
適合者，標示在答案紙上。

Question 26

```
┌─────────────────────────────┐
│     BUSINESS HOURS          │
│      8:30-20:30             │
└─────────────────────────────┘
```

26. Where do you often see this sign?

A. In a hospital.

B. At a school.

C. In an airport.

D. At a stationery store.

請 翻 頁 ▯▭▷

Questions 27-29

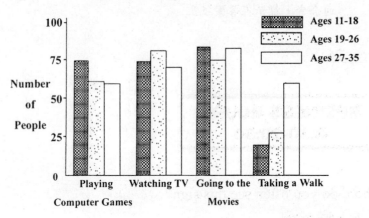

Favourite Things To Do (by age)

27. People aged 11-18 least enjoyed _____.

  A. taking a walk

  B. watching TV

  C. going to the movies

  D. playing computer games

28. What did most people enjoy doing?

  A. Watching TV and playing computer games.

  B. Playing computer games and taking a walk.

  C. Taking a walk and going to the movies.

  D. Going to the movies and watching TV.

29. Which of these sentences is true?
    A. People aged 27-35 enjoyed playing computer games most.
    B. People aged 11-18 enjoyed going to the movies most.
    C. People aged 19-26 enjoyed playing computer games more than watching TV.
    D. Most people like watching TV.

Question 30

Please Notice

We will be closed October 1st to December 15th. Please come back and visit then.

Apple Bookstore

30. How many days will Apple Bookstore be closed?
    A. About 75 days.
    B. About 105 days.
    C. About 45 days.
    D. About 135 days.

請 翻 頁 ⫸

Questions 31-32

★ *Movie Guide* ★

Rush Hour	15:00 23:00	**My Life as Mcdull**	09:00 13:00
Action Movie Do you like Jackie Chan? Rush Hour is his latest movie. It's so exciting. Come and have fun!		Cartoon Mcdull is a little pig. He's kind of silly, but he's very cute. Do you want to share his happiness? Be sure to see it.	
Mr. Bean	11:00 19:00	**Harry Potter III**	17:00 21:00
Comedy Rowan Atkinson is a great actor. His movie Mr. Bean is coming. It's very funny. Don't miss it!		Fantasy（奇幻文學） Harry Potter has been in the wizardry school（魔法學校）for three years. He begins a new adventure. How is everything going?	

31. Molly brings her 6-year-old boy to a movie. Which movie would he most likely want to see?
    A. Rush Hour.   B. My Life as Mcdull.
    C. Mr. Bean.   D. Harry Potter III.

32. It's 17:30 now and you are not allowed to arrive home after 22:00. So, which movie can you see?
    A. Rush Hour.   B. My Life as Mcdull.
    C. Mr. Bean.   D. Harry Potter III.

Questions 33-35

Chinese have a very special way to celebrate the New Year. They light firecrackers and fireworks. The noise is very loud, the smoke is heavy in the air, and the sky is filled with bright rockets.

People say this custom started in ancient times. People back then were afraid of a monster called Nian. Of course, there are no such things as monsters, but people many centuries ago believed there were. They believed this frightening beast would come to try to eat them on New Year's.

They also believed that the monster Nian was afraid of loud noises. So every Chinese New Year, all over the world, wherever there are Chinese people living, you will be able to hear and see fireworks.

請 翻 頁 ◖▭▭▷

33. Firecrackers are similar to small _____.

A. airplanes

B. monsters

C. bombs

D. fires

34. Ancient Chinese believed that _____.

A. Nian would steal their food

B. fireworks would bring good weather

C. a loud noise would bring a lucky New Year

D. there was an evil monster on the earth

35. This holiday story about Nian the monster is _____.

A. very modern

B. extremely old

C. now a famous movie

D. now almost forgotten

初級英語聽力檢定 ① 詳解

一、聽力測驗

第一部份

For questions number 1 and 2, please look at picture A.

1. (**C**) Where are these students?
   A. In a forest.　　　B. At the playground.
   C. On a grassy hill.

   * forest ('fɔrɪst) *n.* 森林
     playground ('ple,graʊnd) *n.* 操場；遊樂場
     grassy ('græsɪ) *adj.* 多草的　　hill (hɪl) *n.* 山丘

2. (**C**) Please look at picture A again. What are they doing?
   A. They are exercising.
   B. They are playing ball.
   C. They are sitting in a circle.

   * exercise ('ɛksə,saɪz) *v.* 運動　　play (ple) *v.* 打 (球)
     ball (bɔl) *n.* 球　　circle ('sɝkl) *n.* 圓圈

For question number 3, please look at picture B.

3. (**A**) What is happening in this picture?
   A. The student is dreaming.
   B. She is hoping for 100 dollars.
   C. The girl is bored.

   * happen ('hæpən) *v.* 發生　　dream (drim) *v.* 作夢
     hope (hop) *v.* 希望　　***hope for*** 希望；期待
     bored (bord) *adj.* 感到無聊的

For question number 4, please look at picture C.

4. (**A**) Who is waiting in line?
     A. Passengers.   B. Salesmen.
     C. Employees.

    * wait〔wet〕v. 等待   line〔laɪn〕n. 隊伍
     wait in line 排隊等候   passenger〔'pæsṇdʒɚ〕n. 乘客
     salesman〔'selzmən〕n. 售貨員
     employee〔͵ɛmplɔɪ'i〕n. 員工

For question number 5, please look at picture D.

5. (**B**) What is happening here?
     A. He is too fat.   B. The boy is eating.
     C. The refrigerator is full.

    * fat〔fæt〕adj. 胖的
     refrigerator〔rɪ'frɪdʒə͵retɚ〕n. 冰箱
     full〔fʊl〕adj. 滿的

For question number 6, please look at picture E.

6. (**C**) What is the bird doing?
     A. He feels very dirty.
     B. It made the man get wet.
     C. It is flying happily.

    * feel〔fil〕v. 覺得   dirty〔'dɝtɪ〕adj. 髒的
     make〔mek〕v. 使   get〔gɛt〕v. 成為…狀態
     wet〔wɛt〕adj. 濕的
     fly〔flaɪ〕v. 飛 (三態變化為：fly-flew-flown)
     happily〔'hæpɪlɪ〕adv. 高興地

For question number 7, please look at picture F.

7. (**A**) Who is on the bicycle?

    A. The PE teacher is.

    B. He is running in a race.

    C. The student is very hot.

    * PE〔'pi'i〕*n.* 體育（= *physical education*）
    run〔rʌn〕*v.* 跑（三態變化爲：run-ran-run）
    race〔res〕*n.* 賽跑　　hot〔hɑt〕*adj.* 熱的

For question number 8, please look at picture G.

8. (**C**) What is John doing?

    A. He is doing well.

    B. Two boys are behind.

    C. He is jumping.

    * *do well* 表現好　　behind〔bɪ'haɪnd〕*adv.* 在後面
    jump〔dʒʌmp〕*v.* 跳

For question number 9, please look at picture H.

9. (**A**) Where is the paint?

    A. In his hand.

    B. He is a painter.

    C. The fence is white.

    * paint〔pent〕*n.* 油漆　　hand〔hænd〕*n.* 手
    painter〔'pentɚ〕*n.* 油漆匠
    fence〔fɛns〕*n.* 籬笆；圍牆
    white〔hwaɪt〕*adj.* 白色的

For question number 10, please look at picture I.

10. (**B**) How will Thursday be?

  A. It will rain.

  B. The weather will be sunny.

  C. It's summertime.

  * weather ('wɛðɚ) *n.* 天氣

  forecast (for'kæst) *n.* (天氣) 預報

  Thursday ('θɝzdɪ) *n.* 星期四 rain (ren) *v.* 下雨

  sunny ('sʌnɪ) *adj.* 晴朗的

  summertime ('sʌmɚ,taɪm) *n.* 夏季

第二部份

11. (**C**) Is it noon yet?

  A. Yes, it's your turn. B. Yes, it's 12:00 a.m.

  C. No, it's only eleven a.m.

  * noon (nun) *n.* 正午 yet (jɛt) *adv.* 已經 (用於疑問句)

  turn (tɝn) *n.* 輪流順序 ***It's your turn.*** 輪到你了。

  a.m. ('e'ɛm) *adv.* 上午 (= *A.M.*)

  12:00 a.m. 凌晨十二點

12. (**A**) Where is that delicious smell coming from?

  A. It must be from the bakery.

  B. I made it myself.

  C. It came from Tainan last night.

  * delicious (dɪ'lɪʃəs) *adj.* 美味的 smell (smɛl) *n.* 氣味

  come from 來自 bakery ('bekərɪ) *n.* 麵包店

  make (mek) *v.* 做 myself (maɪ'sɛlf) *pron.* 我自己

  Tainan 台南 ***last night*** 昨晚

13. (**B**) Can you bowl?

　　A. They're on the second shelf.

　　B. Yes, but not very well.

　　C. No, I couldn't eat another bowl.

　　* bowl〔bol〕v. 打保齡球　n. 碗
　　　second〔'sɛkənd〕adj. 第二的
　　　shelf〔ʃɛlf〕n. 架子　　well〔wɛl〕adv. 很好
　　　another〔ə'nʌðɚ〕adj. 另一個；再一的

14. (**B**) Which of those girls is your cousin?

　　A. Yes, one of them is.

　　B. The one on the left.

　　C. I have a very large family.

　　* which〔hwɪtʃ〕pron. 哪一個
　　　cousin〔'kʌzn̩〕n. 表（堂）兄弟姊妹
　　　left〔lɛft〕n. 左邊
　　　large〔lɑrdʒ〕adj. 大的

15. (**B**) I'm going to buy a dozen doughnuts.

　　A. Are you sure that will be enough for one person?

　　B. But we only need ten.

　　C. The chocolate ones are better.

　　* dozen〔'dʌzn̩〕n. 一打
　　　doughnut〔'do͵nʌt〕n. 甜甜圈（= donut）
　　　sure〔ʃur〕adj. 確定的　　enough〔ə'nʌf〕adj. 足夠的
　　　need〔nid〕v. 需要　　chocolate〔'tʃɔkəlɪt〕adj. 巧克力的
　　　better〔'bɛtɚ〕adj. 比較好的

16. (**C**) Did you get here early today?

    A. No, I always take a taxi.

    B. Yes, we're nearly there.

    C. Yes, at six a.m.

    * get〔gɛt〕v. 抵達　　take〔tek〕v. 搭乘（交通工具）
      nearly〔'nɪrlɪ〕adv. 幾乎

17. (**B**) Have you ever heard of this actor?

    A. No, I haven't heard from him.

    B. Of course. He's famous.

    C. I'm sorry. He's not here now.

    * ever〔'ɛvɚ〕adv. 曾經　　***hear of*** 聽說過…
      actor〔'æktɚ〕n. 男演員　　***hear from***… 得到…的消息
      of course 當然　　famous〔'feməs〕adj. 有名的

18. (**C**) Do you think you can fix this radio?

    A. Yes, I think it's a great price.

    B. I put it in the closet.

    C. No, I'm afraid it's beyond repair.

    * think〔θɪŋk〕v. 認為　　fix〔fɪks〕v. 修理
      radio〔'redɪ,o〕n. 收音機　　great〔gret〕adj. 很棒的
      price〔praɪs〕n. 價格　　put〔pʊt〕v. 放
      closet〔'klɑzɪt〕n. 衣櫥
      afraid〔ə'fred〕adj. 害怕的；擔心的
      beyond〔bɪ'jɑnd〕prep. …所不能及；超過…的範圍
      repair〔rɪ'pɛr〕n. 修理　　***beyond repair*** 無法修理

19. (**A**) Would you like hot coffee or cold?

A. Either one will do. 　　B. No, I'm not cold.

C. Yes, I would.

* cold〔kold〕 *adj.* 冷的　　either〔'iðə〕 *adj.* 兩者任一
Either one will do. 都可以。

20. (**B**) Did you forget to bring your umbrella?

A. Of course you may. Here you are.

B. No, it's right here. 　　C. Sorry. I'll close it.

* forget〔fə'gɛt〕 *v.* 忘記
bring〔brɪŋ〕 *v.* 帶來 (三態變化為 : bring-brought-brought)
umbrella〔ʌm'brɛlə〕 *n.* 雨傘
of course 當然　　may〔me〕 *aux.* 可以
Here you are. 你要的東西在這裡；拿去吧。 (= *Here it is.*)
right〔raɪt〕 *adv.* 正好；恰好　　***right here*** 就在這裡
close〔kloz〕 *v.* 關上

第三部份

21. (**A**) W：I wish I could play an instrument.

M：Don't you play the piano?

W：Yes, but not well.

Question：What is true about the woman?

A. She cannot play an instrument well.

B. She has never played the piano.

C. She can play only the piano well.

* wish〔wɪʃ〕 *v.* 希望　　play〔ple〕 *v.* 演奏；彈
instrument〔'ɪnstrəmənt〕 *n.* 樂器
piano〔pɪ'æno〕 *n.* 鋼琴

22. (**B**) M: Is Jill at home?

W: No, I'm afraid she isn't.

M: Will you tell her I came by?

W: Of course. She should be home soon.

Question: What does the woman mean?

A. She is afraid of the man.

B. She will give Jill the message.

C. She is afraid that Jill will come home soon.

* afraid〔ə'fred〕*adj.* 恐怕…的；害怕的

come by 路過；順路到   soon〔sun〕*adv.* 馬上；很快地

mean〔min〕*v.* 意思是   ***be afraid of*** 害怕

give〔gɪv〕*v.* 給   message〔'mɛsɪdʒ〕*n.* 信息；留言

23. (**C**) M: Why didn't you choose Jack for your team?

W: I'd rather not work with him.

M: I'm surprised. I thought you were good friends.

W: We are, but he's not very hard-working.

Question: Why didn't the woman choose Jack?

A. She thinks he is not a good friend.

B. He is hard to get along with.

C. She thinks he might be lazy.

* choose〔tʃuz〕*v.* 選擇   ***choose…for***~ 選擇…作為~

team〔tim〕*n.* 隊員   ***would rather not V.*** 寧願不要~

surprised〔sə'praɪzd〕*adj.* 驚訝的

think〔θɪŋk〕*v.* 認為 (三態變化為：think-thought-thought)

hard-working〔'hɑrd'wɜkɪŋ〕*adj.* 努力的；用功的

hard〔hɑrd〕*adj.* 困難的   ***get along with*** 相處

might〔maɪt〕*aux.* 可能   lazy〔'lezɪ〕*adj.* 懶惰的

24. (**B**) M : Your little brother is so tall!

    W: Yes, he's grown a lot.

    M: How old is he now?

    W: He's seven.

    Question : What is true about the woman's brother?

    A. He is not yet seven.

    B. He is taller than he was last year.

    C. He is the tallest in his family.

    * tall〔tɔl〕*adj.* 高的 grow〔gro〕*v.* 成長

     a lot 多地 (當副詞) seven〔'sɛvən〕*n.* 七歲

     true〔tru〕*adj.* 正確的 ***not yet*** 尚未

     He is taller than he was last year. 他比去年高。

25. (**B**) W: Oh! This box is so heavy.

    M: Let me help you with it.

    W: Thank you. That's very considerate of you.

    Question : What does the woman think of the man?

    A. He is very strong.

    B. He is very kind.

    C. He is very brave.

    * oh〔o〕*interj.* 喔 (因驚訝所發出的感嘆)

     box〔baks〕*n.* 箱子 heavy〔'hɛvɪ〕*adj.* 重的

     let〔lɛt〕*v.* 讓 ***help sb. with*** sth. 幫忙某人做某事

     considerate〔kən'sɪdərɪt〕*adj.* 體貼的

     think of 認為 strong〔strɔŋ〕*adj.* 強壯的

     kind〔kaɪnd〕*adj.* 仁慈的 brave〔brev〕*adj.* 勇敢的

26. (**B**)　W：Are you ready to mail your letter?

M：I will be as soon as I find an envelope.

W：You can buy one at the shop on the corner.

Question：Where will the man go next?

A. To the post office.

B. To a store.

C. To the shopping mall.

* ready〔'rɛdɪ〕*adj.* 準備好的　　mail〔mel〕*v.* 郵寄
letter〔'lɛtɚ〕*n.* 信　　***as soon as*** 一…就～
find〔faɪnd〕*v.* 找到　　envelope〔'ɛnvə,lop〕*n.* 信封
shop〔ʃɑp〕*n.* 商店　　corner〔'kɔrnɚ〕*n.* 轉角
next〔nɛkst〕*adv.* 接著　　***post office*** 郵局
store〔stor〕*n.* 商店　　mall〔mɔl〕*n.* 購物中心
shopping mall 購物中心

27. (**B**)　M：This telephone number can't be right.

W：What's wrong?

M：There are only six numbers.

W：Sorry. I must have omitted one.

Question：What did the woman do?

A. She erased one of the numbers.

B. She forgot to write one of the numbers.

C. She could not remember the telephone number.

* telephone〔'tɛlə,fon〕*n.* 電話
number〔'nʌmbɚ〕*n.* 號碼　　right〔raɪt〕*adj.* 正確的
What's wrong? 怎麼了？　　omit〔o'mɪt〕*v.* 遺漏
erase〔ɪ'res〕*v.* 擦掉　　remember〔rɪ'mɛmbɚ〕*v.* 記得

28. (**C**) W：The box is in the closet, on the top shelf.

M：I can't see it.

W：Here. Use this flashlight.

M：Ah. There it is.

Question：Why couldn't the man see the box?

A. He was not tall enough.

B. He was looking on the wrong shelf.

C. The closet was too dark.

* closet ('klɑzɪt) n. 衣櫥   top (tɑp) adj. 最上面的
  shelf (ʃɛlf) n. 架子 (複數為 shelves (ʃɛlvz))
  here (hɪr) interj. 喂 (用於引起別人的注意)
  use (juz) v. 使用；利用   flashlight ('flæʃ,laɪt) n. 手電筒
  ah (ɑ) interj. 啊   *There it is.* 在那裡。
  wrong (rɔŋ) adj. 錯誤的   dark (dɑrk) adj. 暗的

29. (**A**) M：Oh, no! I forgot about the test today!

W：You mean you didn't study at all?

M：No, and it's too late now.

W：Then you had better start praying.

Question：What does the woman suggest?

A. That the man ask God for help.

B. That the man prepare for the test right away.

C. That the man start studying sooner next time.

* *Oh, no!* 噢，糟了！   test (tɛst) n. 測驗
  not…at all 一點也不   late (let) adj. 遲的
  had better V. 最好～   pray (pre) v. 祈禱
  suggest (səg'dʒɛst) v. 建議
  ask sb. for help 請求某人的幫助   God (gɑd) n. 上帝
  prepare (prɪ'pɛr) v. 準備   *right away* 馬上
  sooner ('sunɚ) adv. 較早地 (soon 的比較級)
  next time 下一次

30. (**B**) W: What did you like most about your trip to Canada?

M: I liked learning to ski.

W: What else?

M: I also made a snowman.

Question: When did the man go abroad?

A. He went to Canada.

B. He went during the winter.

C. His parents made him go.

* trip〔trɪp〕*n.* 旅行

Canada〔'kænədə〕*n.* 加拿大

learn〔lɜn〕*v.* 學習　ski〔ski〕*v.* 滑雪

What else? 還有呢？

make〔mek〕*v.* 做；使…（做～）

snowman〔'sno,mæn〕*n.* 雪人

abroad〔ə'brɔd〕*adv.* 到國外

during〔'djʊrɪŋ〕*prep.* 在…期間

winter〔'wɪntɚ〕*n.* 冬天

parents〔'pɛrənts〕*n. pl.* 父母

二、閱讀能力測驗

第一部份：詞彙和結構

1. (**A**) I was tired, so I <u>lay</u> down on the sofa and slept.
   我很累，所以躺在沙發上睡覺。

   > lie「躺」的三態變化爲：lie-lay-lain，依句意爲過去式，
   > 故選 (A) lay。而 (B) laid 是 lay「下蛋；放置」的過去
   > 式，(D) lied 是 lie「說謊」的過去式。

   * tired〔taɪrd〕*adj.* 疲倦的　　sofa〔'sofə〕*n.* 沙發

2. (**A**) "Ian, you never learned to drive, <u>did you</u>?"
   「伊安，你從沒學過開車，<u>是嗎？</u>」

   > 附加問句與敘述句的動詞時態須相同（learned 爲過去
   > 式），且敘述句是否定（有 never）時，附加問句應爲肯
   > 定，故應選 (A) did you。

   * drive〔draɪv〕*v.* 開車

3. (**C**) I want to learn painting <u>during</u> my vacation in Taipei.
   我想在台北度假<u>期間</u>學繪畫。

   (A) while〔hwaɪl〕*conj.* 當…的時候
   (B) until〔ən'tɪl〕*prep.* 直到…爲止
   (C) ***during***〔'djurɪŋ〕*prep.* 在…期間
   (D) for〔fɔr〕*prep.* 在…期間（一直）；持續（多久）

   > (A) 是連接詞，後應接子句，(B) 後應接一時間點，(D)
   > 是強調動作持續的期間，故應選 (C) 表某一特定的期間。

   * painting〔'pentɪŋ〕*n.* 繪畫
   　vacation〔ve'keʃən〕*n.* 假期

4. (**D**) The notice was written <u>with</u> a crayon.

這公告是<u>用</u>蠟筆寫的。

　　(A) be written from… …寫來的（信）
　　(B) be written in… 被寫進…（書）中
　　(C) write of… 寫關於…
　　(D) ***write with***… 用…寫

　　* notice〔'notɪs〕 *n.* 告示
　　crayon〔'kreən〕 *n.* 蠟筆

5. (**C**) Your son will be <u>a</u> Mozart in the future.

你的兒子將來會成為<u>一位像莫札特一樣的音樂家</u>。

　　「a(n)＋名人」表「像名人一樣的人」，故選 (C)。

　　* Mozart〔'mozɑrt〕 *n.* 莫札特
　　future〔'fjutʃɚ〕 *n.* 未來

6. (**A**) I have two English dictionaries; one is big and <u>the other</u> is small.

我有兩本英文字典；一本是大的，<u>另一本</u>是小的。

　　要分別說明前面提及的兩個人事物時，一個用 one 代替，另一個則用 ***the other*** 代替，故選 (A)。

　　* dictionary〔'dɪkʃən,ɛrɪ〕 *n.* 字典

7. (**C**) The lady <u>whom</u> Iris lives with is my sister.

和愛瑞絲住在一起的女士是我的姊妹。

　　先行詞 The lady 做介系詞 with 的受詞，故關係代名詞要用受格 whom，選 (C)。

8. (**C**) If I had taken your advice then, I <u>would have finished</u> the work now.

如果那時我有接受你的忠告，現在我<u>將已經完成</u>工作了。

由條件句的「過去完成式」可知，這是一個「與過去事實相反」的假設法句型，故主要子句須用「would/should/could/might + have + 過去分詞」，故選 (C)。

* advice〔əd'vaɪs〕*n.* 忠告
  take one's advice 接受某人忠告　　finish〔'fɪnɪʃ〕*v.* 完成

9. (**B**) I will wait in the rain until Sara <u>opens</u> the door.

我會在雨中一直等到莎拉<u>開</u>門。

表「時間」的副詞子句中，應以現在代替未來，故選 (B)。

* ***in the rain*** 在雨中　　until〔ən'tɪl〕*conj.* 直到

10. (**D**) Stop <u>playing</u> that video game! Have you finished your homework? 不要再<u>打</u>電動了！你功課做完了嗎？

$\begin{cases} \text{stop} + \text{V-ing} & \text{停止做～（動作已做）} \\ \text{stop} + \text{to V.} & \text{停下來去做～（動作未做）} \end{cases}$

* ***video game*** 電動玩具

11. (**D**) This closet was <u>made of</u> a teak wood, so it's quite expensive.

這個衣櫥是<u>由柚木製成</u>，所以相當昂貴。

$\begin{cases} \text{be made} + \text{from～} & \text{以～製成（材料本質已變）} \\ \text{be made} + \text{of～} & \text{以～製成（材料本質未變）} \end{cases}$

* closet〔'klɑzɪt〕*n.* 衣櫥　　teak〔tik〕*n.* 柚木
  wood〔wʊd〕*n.* 木材　　quite〔kwaɪt〕*adv.* 相當
  expensive〔ɪk'spɛnsɪv〕*adj.* 昂貴的

12. (**D**) I don't want <u>much</u> pepper in my soup. Just a little, please. 我的湯不要<u>很多</u>胡椒粉。請放一點點就好。

> 由第二句知，並非完全不要胡椒粉，且 pepper（胡椒粉）為不可數名詞，故選 (D)。

> * pepper〔'pɛpɚ〕*n.* 胡椒（粉）
> soup〔sup〕*n.* 湯

13. (**D**) She <u>used to be</u> a beautiful girl, but she is an old lady now.
她<u>從前是</u>一個美麗的女孩，但現在是個老太太了。

> $\begin{cases} \textit{\textbf{be used to}} + \textit{\textbf{V-ing}} \,/\, \textit{\textbf{N.}} \quad 習慣於～ \\ \textit{\textbf{used to be}} + \textit{\textbf{N.}} \quad 從前是～ \end{cases}$

14. (**C**) My bicycle was stolen, so I have to go home <u>on</u> foot.
我的腳踏車被偷了，所以我必須<u>徒步</u>回家。

> with 雖可表「用～」，但「用腳回家」不合理，應選 (C)，形成 *on foot*「徒步」。

> * steal〔stil〕*v.* 偷（三態變化為：steal-stole-stolen）
> *on foot* 徒步

15. (**A**) Amy will leave <u>for</u> Paris next week. There will be big sales in Paris then.
艾咪下星期要去巴黎。那時巴黎會有大減價特賣。

> $\begin{cases} \textit{\textbf{leave for}}～ \quad 前往～ \\ \textit{\textbf{leave from}}～ \quad 從～離開 \end{cases}$

> * Paris〔'pærɪs〕*n.* 巴黎　　sale〔sel〕*n.* 特價；拍賣
> then〔ðɛn〕*adv.* 那時

第二部份：段落填空

Questions 16-20

Some people try <u>hard</u> to have better things than other people,
　　　　　　　　16

so they <u>borrow</u> money from friendly banks. They can buy
　　　　　17

anything they want, but the money they spend is not <u>theirs</u>. This
　　　　　　　　　　　　　　　　　　　　　　　　18

materialistic (物質主義的) world has <u>influenced</u> our young
　　　　　　　　　　　　　　　　　　　19

generation very much. Some young people use credit cards to

buy things they want. They don't care <u>if</u> they have enough
　　　　　　　　　　　　　　　　　　　20

money to pay back the banks.

　　有些人很努力想擁有比別人更好的東西，所以他們跟友善的銀行借
錢。他們可以買他們想要的任何東西，但是他們花的錢不是他們自己的。
這個物質主義的世界已經對我們年輕的一代，造成很大的影響。有些年
輕人用信用卡買他們想要的東西，他們不在乎是否有足夠的錢還給銀
行。

> try〔traɪ〕v. 嘗試　　better〔'bɛtɚ〕adj. 更好的
> friendly〔'frɛndlɪ〕adj. 友善的
> bank〔bæŋk〕n. 銀行　　spend〔spɛnd〕v. 花費
> materialistic〔mə,tɪrɪəl'ɪstɪk〕adj. 物質主義的
> generation〔,dʒɛnə'reʃən〕n. 世代
> **credit card** 信用卡　　care〔kɛr〕v. 在乎
> pay〔pe〕v. 付錢　　**pay back** 償還

16. (**B**) (A) hardly (ˈhɑrdlɪ) *adv.* 幾乎不

 (B) ***hard*** (hɑrd) *adv.* 努力地

 (C) often (ˈɔfən) *adv.* 經常

 (D) sincerely (sɪnˈsɪrlɪ) *adv.* 衷心地

17. (**A**) (A) ***borrow*** (ˈbɑro) *v.* 借 (入)

 (B) lend (lɛnd) *v.* 借 (出)

 (C) bring (brɪŋ) *v.* 帶來

 (D) spend (spɛnd) *v.* 花費

18. (**A**) 依句意，選 (A) they 的所有格代名詞 ***theirs*** (= *their money*)。而沒有 (B) their's 這種寫法，(C) their 是 they 的所有格，(D) them 是 they 的受格。

19. (**B**) (A) improve (ɪmˈpruv) *v.* 改進

 (B) ***influence*** (ˈɪnfluəns) *v.* 影響

 (C) offer (ˈɔfɚ) *v.* 提供

 (D) puzzle (ˈpʌzl̩) *v.* 使困惑

20. (**D**) 按照句意，他們不在乎「是否」有足夠的錢還銀行，故選 (D) ***if*** 「是否」。

Questions 21-25

I'm fond of <u>writing</u> emails to people from other countries.
         21

My favorite online friend lives in Italy. I <u>sent</u> a letter to him
                                 22

two weeks ago. I haven't received an answer to that letter <u>yet</u>.
                                      23

Maybe my English is <u>so</u> poor that he didn't understand what
                     24

I <u>wrote</u>.
  25

我很喜歡寫電子郵件給其他國家的人。我最喜歡的網友住在義大
利。兩個星期前我寄了一封信給他，我還沒收到他對那封信的回應，
可能是我的英文太爛了，他不懂我在寫什麼。

    be fond of 喜歡 (= *like*)
    email ('i‚mel) *n.* 電子郵件 (= *e-mail*)
    country ('kʌntrɪ) *n.* 國家
    favorite ('fevərɪt) *adj.* 最喜愛的
    online ('ɑn‚laɪn) *adj.* 線上的；網路上的 (= *on-line*)
    online friend 網友   Italy ('ɪtḷɪ) *n.* 義大利
    letter ('lɛtɚ) *n.* 信   answer ('ænsɚ) *n.* 回覆；回答
    maybe ('mebɪ) *adv.* 或許   poor (pur) *adj.* 差的

21. (**C**) be fond of 後若接動詞，應改為動名詞的形式，因 of 是介系
      詞，故選 (C) ***writing***。

22. (**A**) 現在完成式不能與「表過去確定的時間副詞」連用，本句句
      尾有 two weeks ago，故須用過去式，選 (A) ***sent***。
      * send (sɛnd) *v.* 寄；送

23. (**D**) (A) still 作「仍然」解時，通常置於句中；(B) really「眞正地」通常置於句中；(C) already「已經」只能用於肯定句；(D) yet 用在疑問句時，作「已經」解，用在「否定句」時，作「尚（未）」解，通常置於句尾，故依句意，選 (D) *yet*。

24. (**B**) 由形容詞 poor 後的 that 及句意得知，應選(B) *so*，來形成 so…that～「如此…以致於～」的句型。

25. (**D**) 這封信是過去寫的，故 (A) 不合；寫信的動作已完成，並無繼續的意味，亦非剛完成的動作，故不可用現在完成式，故 (B) 不合；複合關係代名詞 what 應引導一子句，若選 (C) 則不成子句（沒有動詞）；故應選簡單過去式 (D) *wrote*。

第三部份：閱讀理解

Question 26

```
┌─────────────────────────┐
│   營 業 時 間            │
│   8:30-20:30            │
└─────────────────────────┘
```

26. (**D**) 你常常在哪裡看到這個告示牌？

    (A) 在醫院。   (B) 在學校。

    (C) 在機場。   (D) <u>在文具店。</u>

    * hours〔aʊrz〕*n. pl.* 時間   sign〔saɪn〕*n.* 告示牌
      hospital〔'hɑspɪtl〕*n.* 醫院
      airport〔'ɛr,port〕*n.* 機場
      stationery〔'steʃən,ɛrɪ〕*n.* 文具

Questions 27-29

Favourite Things To Do (by age)

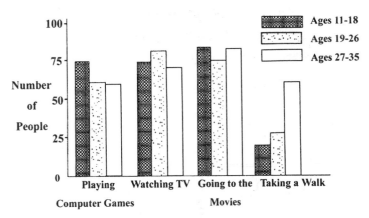

favorite〔'fevərɪt〕adj. 最喜愛的　　age〔edʒ〕n. 年齡
number〔'nʌmbɚ〕n. 人數
computer games 電動玩具；電玩遊戲
go to the movie 去看電影　　*take a walk* 散步

27. (**A**) 十一至十八歲的人最不喜歡_____。

　　(A) 散步　　　　　　　(B) 看電視
　　(C) 看電影　　　　　　(D) 打電動
　　* aged〔edʒd〕adj. …歲的　　least〔list〕adv. 最不
　　　enjoy〔ɪn'dʒɔɪ〕v. 喜歡；享受

28. (**D**) 什麼是大多數的人喜歡做的？

　　(A) 看電視和打電動。　　(B) 打電動和散步。
　　(C) 散步和看電影。　　　(D) 看電影和看電視。
　　* most〔most〕adj. 大多數的

29. (**B**) 哪一個句子是正確的？

    (A) 二十七至三十五歲的人最喜歡打電動。

    (B) <u>十一至十八歲的人最喜歡看電影。</u>

    (C) 十九至二十六歲的人喜歡打電動甚於看電視。

    (D) 大多數的人喜歡看電視。

    * sentence〔'sɛntəns〕*n.* 句子

Question 30

> # 請 注 意
> ◆
> 我們將從十月一日休
> 息至十二月十五日。請
> 屆時再回來參觀選購。
>
> 蘋果書店

notice〔'notɪs〕*v.* 注意   close〔kloz〕*v.* 歇業

October〔ɑk'tobɚ〕*n.* 十月

December〔dɪ'sɛmbɚ〕*n.* 十二月

visit〔'vɪzɪt〕*v.* 參觀；去   then〔ðɛn〕*adv.* 屆時；到那時

bookstore〔'bʊk,stor〕*n.* 書店

30. (**A**) 蘋果書店將歇業幾天？

    (A) <u>約七十五天。</u>   (B) 約一百零五天。

    (C) 約四十五天。   (D) 約一百三十五天。

Questions 31-32

★ 電影指南 ★

尖峰時刻	15:00 23:00	麥兜的故事	09:00 13:00
動作片 　你喜歡成龍嗎？「尖峰時刻」是他最新的電影。相當刺激，來好好享受吧！		**卡通** 　麥兜是一隻小豬，他有點笨，但是他非常可愛。你想要分享他的快樂嗎？一定要來看哦。	
豆豆先生	11:00 19:00	哈利波特第三集	17:00 21:00
喜劇 　羅溫艾金森是一個偉大的演員。他的電影「豆豆先生」來了。它很有趣，別錯過了！		**奇幻文學** 　哈利波特已經在魔法學校三年了，他開始了新的冒險。一切進展得如何呢？	

guide〔gaɪd〕n. 指南　　rush〔rʌʃ〕adj. 匆忙的

rush hour 尖峰時間　　action〔'ækʃən〕n. 動作

Jackie Chan 成龍　　latest〔'letɪst〕adj. 最新的

exciting〔ɪk'saɪtɪŋ〕adj. 刺激的　　***have fun*** 玩得開心

cartoon〔kɑr'tun〕n. 卡通　　***kind of*** 有一點

silly〔'sɪlɪ〕adj. 愚蠢的　　cute〔kjut〕adj. 可愛的

share〔ʃɛr〕v. 分享　　sure〔ʃʊr〕adj. 確定的；一定的

bean〔bin〕n. 豆子　　comedy〔'kɑmədɪ〕n. 喜劇

actor〔'æktɚ〕n. 男演員　　funny〔'fʌnɪ〕adj. 好笑的

miss〔mɪs〕v. 錯過　　fantasy〔'fæntəsɪ〕n. 奇幻文學

wizardry〔'wɪzɚdrɪ〕n. 巫術　　begin〔bɪ'gɪn〕n. 開始

adventure〔əd'vɛntʃɚ〕n. 冒險　　go〔go〕v. 進展

31. (**B**) 茉莉帶著她六歲的兒子去看電影。他很可能最想看哪部電影？

(A) 尖峰時刻。   (B) <u>麥兜的故事。</u>

(C) 豆豆先生。   (D) 哈利波特第三集。

* bring〔brɪŋ〕v. 帶   **6-year-old** 六歲的

likely〔'laɪklɪ〕adv. 可能地

32. (**C**) 現在是下午五點半，你不可以在晚上十點以後到家。那麼，你可以看哪部電影？

(A) 尖峰時刻。   (B) 麥兜的故事。

(C) <u>豆豆先生。</u>   (D) 哈利波特第三集。

* allow〔ə'laʊ〕v. 允許   arrive〔ə'raɪv〕v. 到達

Questions 33-35

Chinese have a very special way to celebrate the New Year. They light firecrackers and fireworks. The noise is very loud, the smoke is heavy in the air, and the sky is filled with bright rockets.

中國人有一個非常特別的方式慶祝新年，他們燃放鞭炮和煙火。
聲音很大，空氣中濃煙密佈，天空中滿是燦爛的煙火。

special〔'spɛʃəl〕adj. 特別的   way〔we〕n. 方式；方法

celebrate〔'sɛlə,bret〕v. 慶祝   light〔laɪt〕v. 點燃

firecracker〔'faɪr,krækɚ〕n. 鞭炮

firework〔'faɪr,wɝk〕n. 煙火   noise〔nɔɪz〕n. 聲響；噪音

loud〔laʊd〕adj. 大聲的   smoke〔smok〕n. 煙

heavy〔'hɛvɪ〕adj. 濃密的   air〔ɛr〕n. 空氣

in the air 在空中   sky〔skaɪ〕n. 天空   fill〔fɪl〕v. 裝滿

be filled with 充滿了   bright〔braɪt〕adj. 明亮的

rocket〔'rɑkɪt〕n. 沖天煙火

People say this custom started in ancient times. People back then were afraid of a monster called Nian. Of course, there are no such things as monsters, but people many centuries ago believed there were. They believed this frightening beast would come to try to eat them on New Year's.

聽說這個習俗開始於古代。那時候的人害怕一隻叫「年」的怪獸。當然沒有怪獸這回事，但是幾世紀以前的人相信有。他們相信，這嚇人的野獸會在新年時前來，想要吃掉他們。

custom〔'kʌstəm〕n. 習俗　　start〔stɑrt〕v. 開始
ancient〔'enʃənt〕adj. 古代的　　times〔taɪmz〕n. pl. 時代
back〔bæk〕adv. 過去　　then〔ðɛn〕adv. 那時
afraid〔ə'fred〕adj. 害怕的　　**be afraid of** 害怕
monster〔'mɑnstɚ〕n. 怪獸　　**called~** 叫作~
as〔əz〕prep. 如… ; 像…　　century〔'sɛntʃərɪ〕n. 世紀
ago〔ə'go〕adv. …之前　　believe〔bɪ'liv〕v. 相信
frightening〔'fraɪtn̩ɪŋ〕adj. 可怕的　　beast〔bist〕n. 野獸

They also believed that the monster Nian was afraid of loud noises. So every Chinese New Year, all over the world, wherever there are Chinese people living, you will be able to hear and see fireworks.

他們也相信，這年獸害怕吵雜的噪音。所以，每次的中國新年，在世界各地，只要有中國人住的地方，你就能聽到，並且看到煙火。

all over 遍及　　wherever〔hwɛr'ɛvɚ〕conj. 無論何地
be able to 能夠

33. (**C**)　鞭炮類似於小型的＿＿＿＿＿。

    (A) airplane（'ɛr,plen）*n.* 飛機

    (B) monster（'mɑnstɚ）*n.* 怪獸

    (C) ***bomb***（bɑm）*n.* 炸彈

    (D) fire（faɪr）*n.* 火

    * similar（'sɪmələ）*adj.* 類似的

34. (**D**)　古代的中國人相信＿＿＿＿＿。

    (A)「年」會偷他們的食物

    (B) 煙火會帶來好天氣

    (C) 吵雜的噪音會帶來幸運的一年

    (D) <u>地球上有一隻邪惡的怪獸</u>

    * steal（stil）*v.* 偷　　bring（brɪŋ）*v.* 帶來

      weather（'wɛðɚ）*n.* 天氣　　lucky（'lʌkɪ）*adj.* 幸運的

      evil（'ivḷ）*adj.* 邪惡的　　earth（ɝθ）*n.* 地球

35. (**B**)　這個關於年的這隻怪獸的節日故事＿＿＿＿＿。

    (A) 是非常現代的

    (B) <u>是相當古老的</u>

    (C) 現在是一部著名的電影

    (D) 現在幾乎被忘記了

    * holiday（'hɑlə,de）*n.* 節日

      modern（'mɑdɚn）*adj.* 現代的

      extremely（ɪk'strimlɪ）*adv.* 非常；極度地

      famous（'feməs）*adj.* 有名的

      almost（'ɔl,most）*adv.* 幾乎

      forget（fɚ'gɛt）*v.* 忘記

全民英語能力分級檢定測驗
初級測驗 ②

一、聽力測驗

本測驗分三部份，全爲三選一之選擇題，每部份各 10 題，共 30 題，作答時間約 20 分鐘。

第一部份：看圖辨義

本部份共 10 題，試題冊上每題有一個圖片，請聽錄音機播出一個相關的問題，與 A、B、C 三個英語敘述後，選一個與所看到圖片最相符的答案，並在答案紙上相對的圓圈內塗黑作答。每題播出一遍，問題及選項均不印在試題冊上。

例：（看）

NT$80   NT$50

（聽）

Look at the picture. How much is the hamburger?

 A. It's eighty dollars.

 B. It's fifty-five dollars.

 C. It's eighteen dollars.

正確答案爲 A

Question 1

Question 2

Question 3

Question 4

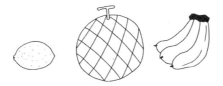

Question 5

請 翻 頁 ▮⟹

Question 6

Question 7

Question 8

Question 9

Question 10

請 翻 頁 ⟹

第二部份：問答

本部份共 10 題，每題錄音機會播出一個問句或直述句，每題播出一次，聽後請從試題冊上 A、B、C 三個選項中，選出一個最適合的回答或回應，並在答案紙上塗黑作答。

例：

（聽）　Good morning, Kevin.　How are you?

（看）　A.　I'm fine, thank you.
　　　　B.　I'm in the living room.
　　　　C.　My name is Kevin.

正確答案為 A

11. A. Yes, you may lend it.
　　B. Sorry, but this is my only one.
　　C. What color is it?

12. A. I will marry next year.
　　B. It was at 2:00.
　　C. My brother's.

13. A. Through the window.
　　B. There were two of them.
　　C. About fifty thousand.

14. A. No, not a soul.
　　B. Yes, it's raining.
　　C. Go two blocks and turn left.

15. A. The maximum
    number of passengers
    is 18.
    B. We have a special
    price for large groups.
    C. It will leave when
    full.

16. A. Yes, a storm is
    coming.
    B. No, I haven't heard
    from her.
    C. No, I don't care for it.

17. A. It's my favorite song,
    too.
    B. It's delicious.
    C. Thank you. It's new.

18. A. Most people like to
    go shopping.
    B. About one million.
    C. Yes, we have many
    visitors.

19. A. They play popular
    music.
    B. There are four.
    C. There is a piano
    in it.

20. A. Yes, I can't wait to
    go.
    B. Yes, I'll pay it right
    away.
    C. No, I haven't made
    a reservation.

請 翻 頁 ▉⟹

第三部份： 簡短對話

　　本部份共 10 題，每題錄音機會播出一段對話及一個相關的問題，每題播出兩次，聽後請從試題冊上 A、B、C 三個選項中，選出一個最適合的回答，並在答案紙上塗黑作答。

例：

（聽）(Woman) Good afternoon, ...Mr. Davis?

　　　(Man)　Yes. I have an appointment with Dr. Sanders at two o'clock. My son Tommy has a fever.

　　　(Woman) Oh, that's too bad. Well, please have a seat, Mr. Davis. Dr. Sanders will be right with you.

　　　Question: Where did this conversation take place?

（看）A. In a post office.

　　　B. In a restaurant.

　　　C. In a doctor's office.

正確答案為 C

21. A. Worried about the test.
    B. Excited about the PE class.
    C. Physically tired.

22. A. He is a student.
    B. He will be a lawyer.
    C. He will have a graduation.

23. A. In one hour.
    B. Japan.
    C. Quickly.

24. A. She ate cereal, too.
    B. She did not eat breakfast.
    C. She eats when she is nervous.

25. A. They are missing.
    B. They are playing together.
    C. They are looking for their parents.

26. A. He is excited about them.
    B. He does not know how to skate yet.
    C. He doesn't like them very much.

請 翻 頁 ॥⟹

27. A. The man must drink
       more tea.
    B. It was a lot of
       trouble to find the
       kettle.
    C. She has already
       started to make tea.

28. A. The woman's
       sister.
    B. The man.
    C. The woman's niece.

29. A. Whether or not the
       woman likes big cities.
    B. Whether or not the
       woman likes living
       in the north.
    C. Whether or not the
       woman's village is
       interesting.

30. A. It is worthless.
    B. It is valuable.
    C. It is closed.

二、閱讀能力測驗

本測驗分三部份,全為四選一之選擇題,共 35 題,作答時間 35 分鐘。

第一部份: 詞彙和結構

本部份共15題,每題含一個空格。請就試題冊上 A、B、C、D 四個選項中選出最適合題意的字或詞,標示在答案紙上。

1. Use the zebra crossing, _____ you will be hit by a car.
   A. and
   B. when
   C. or
   D. for

2. My father had a _____ repair our car.
   A. dentist
   B. journalist
   C. vendor
   D. mechanic

3. Greg _____ the red light and was fined NT$1200.
   A. ignored
   B. illegal
   C. past
   D. drove

請 翻 頁 ⟹

4. You have to _____ a stamp on the envelope before you mail it.
   A. past
   B. paste
   C. post
   D. pack

5. If my pronunciation is wrong, please _____ me.
   A. connect
   B. correct
   C. check
   D. concern

6. He _____ show up on time, or he will be fired.
   A. has better
   B. had better
   C. has better to
   D. was better to

7. Tim   : _____ do you have your car washed?
   Duncan : Once a week.
   A. How far
   B. How soon
   C. How long
   D. How often

8. She _____ on the phone for two hours. Who is she talking to?

　A. talked

　B. has talked

　C. had been talking

　D. has been talking

9. Could you _____ me some money? I lost my wallet.

　A. lend

　B. lend to

　C. borrow

　D. borrow to

10. This pen is different _____ the one I lent you yesterday.

　A. from

　B. of

　C. for

　D. at

11. _____ he saw the police, he started to run away.

　A. As long as

　B. As soon as

　C. As fast as

　D. As well as

請 翻 頁

12. Do you see that man _____ coat is red?
    A. his
    B. that
    C. who
    D. whose

13. It _____ me four hours to write this report.
    A. took
    B. spent
    C. used
    D. cost

14. It's impolite _____ Kate to say dirty words to the teacher.
    A. of
    B. from
    C. at
    D. by

15. Jack heard Spot _____ by his master last night.
    A. scold
    B. was scolding
    C. scolded
    D. scolding

第二部份：段落填空

　　本部份共 10 題，包括二個段落，每個段落各含 5 個空格。請就試題冊上 A、B、C、D 四個選項中選出最適合題意的字或詞，標示在答案紙上。

Questions 16-21

　　It was getting dark. Some children and two Canadian women were still ___(16)___ on the ice. Suddenly the ice broke. One of the boys fell into the water. The children shouted, "Help!" They didn't know ___(17)___ to do.

　　The two Canadian friends heard them and skated ___(18)___ to get the boy out of the water. The ice was ___(19)___ . The two Canadians fell into the water, too. But they tried their best to save the little boy. They knew they must be ___(20)___ , or the boy would soon die. Many people ran over to help. A young man jumped into the water to save the three people. The boy and the two Canadian women were out of the water ___(21)___ .

16. A. boating
    B. skating
    C. planting
    D. swimming

17. A. who
    B. when
    C. what
    D. where

請 翻 頁 ⫸

18. A. ahead
　　B. over
　　C. by
　　D. up

19. A. big
　　B. small
　　C. thick
　　D. thin

20. A. slow
　　B. quick
　　C. sorry
　　D. wrong

21. A. at all
　　B. at least
　　C. at first
　　D. at last

Questions 22-25

　　Our house has two ___(22)___. It has three rooms on the second floor. One is my brother's room, ___(23)___ is our study room, and ___(24)___ is mine. We ___(25)___ in this house for twelve years. I was born and brought up in this house.

22. A. steps
　　B. stairs
　　C. stories
　　D. ceilings

23. A. other
　　B. another
　　C. others
　　D. the other

24. A. other
　　B. another
　　C. others
　　D. the other

25. A. are living
　　B. have lived
　　C. had lived
　　D. live

第三部份：　閱讀理解

本部份共 10 題，包括數段短文，每段短文後有 1～3 個相關問題，請就試題冊上 A、B、C、D 四個選項中選出最適合者，標示在答案紙上。

Questions 26-27

The Sweet House

5/05/2006   7:26 P.M.

Qty.	Item	Price
1	shirt	$390
2	jeans	$890 each
1	belt	$450
Total		$2,620

26. This is a _____ from The Sweet House.
   A. notice
   B. sign
   C. check
   D. receipt

27. Which item might be available at The Sweet House?
   A. Trousers.
   B. Carpet.
   C. Glue.
   D. Robot.

請 翻 頁 ◀▋▭▭⟹

<u>Questions 28-30</u>

Eating the Right Kind of Food

The pyramid（金字塔）below shows what kinds of food
you should eat each day to be healthy.

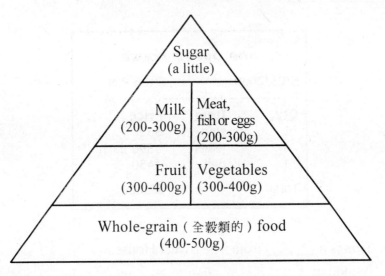

28. What should we eat most each day?
    A. Meat or fish.　　　　　B. Vegetables.
    C. Whole-grain food.　　　D. Fruit.

29. What should we eat the least of?
    A. Milk.　　　　　　　　B. Fruit.
    C. Meat or fish.　　　　　D. Sugar.

30. Which should be eaten more, milk or meat?

　　A. As much milk as meat.

　　B. Not as much meat as milk.

　　C. More milk than meat.

　　D. More meat than milk.

Questions 31-33

Do you celebrate April Fools' Day? In many western countries, on this day, you may play a joke or a funny trick on another person. But your activity must be safe. You must only try to make that person feel foolish. Then you can laugh and yell out "April Fools'."

The history of April Fools' Day is not totally clear. Some believe it came from several different cultures, and their celebrations involving the first day of spring. Some say it started in France, while others believe it began in England or Scotland. No matter where it started, by the eighteenth century, April Fools' Day had become an international fun day.

In early America, one popular trick was to stick a funny note like, "Kick me" or "I'm stupid" on someone's back without them knowing it! Would you ever do that?

請 翻 頁 ◀️⟹

31. What is an important thing about April Fools' Day?

    A. Your trick must be very funny.

    B. Your trick can not cause harm.

    C. You can not lie.

    D. You can not make fun of others.

32. In which part of the world did this holiday probably begin?

    A. Asia.

    B. North America.

    C. The Middle East.

    D. Europe.

33. April Fools' Day is a chance to _____.

    A. start a fire

    B. call someone an idiot

    C. do something humorous

    D. be silly in front of strangers

Questions 34-35

William's Institute（學院）of English

◎ English courses（課程）

◎ Small classes

　(twelve students in each class)

◎ 480 students

◎ 8-week courses

For further information contact（接洽）：
The Headmaster
William's Institute of English
38 Apple Street, London
Telephone: 01-123-4567

---

34. The institute is in _____.

   A. America　　　　　　B. Australia

   C. England　　　　　　D. Canada

35. Who does the institute want to have?

   A. Students.　　　　　B. Teachers.

   C. Workers.　　　　　D. Doctors.

初級英檢模擬試題②詳解

一、聽力測驗

Look at the picture for question 1.

1. (**C**) What is the girl doing?

    A. She is very angry.

    B. He is looking at his watch.

    C. She is waiting.

    * angry〔'æŋgrɪ〕*adj.* 生氣的　　***look at*** 看著
    watch〔wɑtʃ〕*n.* 手錶　　wait〔wet〕*v.* 等待

Look at the picture for question 2.

2. (**B**) Why is the woman taking a picture?

    A. The flowers are beautiful.

    B. It is graduation day.

    C. She likes to be in pictures.

    * picture〔'pɪktʃɚ〕*n.* 照片　　***take a picture*** 照相
    flower〔'flauɚ〕*n.* 花
    graduation〔͵grædʒu'eʃən〕*n.* 畢業

Look at the picture for question 3.

3. (**B**) What is the mother probably saying?

    A. I feel so terrible.

    B. What is the matter, honey?

    C. My pet dog died.

* probably ('prɑbəblɪ) *adv.* 可能　　feel (fil) *v.* 覺得
terrible ('tɛrəbḷ) *adj.* 可怕的；很糟的
What's the matter? 怎麼了？
honey ('hʌnɪ) *n.* 親愛的　　pet (pɛt) *n.* 寵物
die (daɪ) *v.* 死

Look at the picture for question 4.

4. (**C**) Which fruit is the most sour?

    A. Melon and banana.

    B. None of them.

    C. Lemon.

    * which (hwɪtʃ) *adj.* 哪一個　　fruit (frut) *n.* 水果
    sour (saʊr) *adj.* 酸的　　melon ('mɛlən) *n.* 甜瓜
    none of~　~其中都沒有　　lemon ('lɛmən) *n.* 檸檬

Look at the picture for question 5.

5. (**B**) How does the girl feel in her dream?

    A. Cold.　　　　　　B. Scared.

    C. Shaking.

    * dream (drim) *n.* 夢　　cold (kold) *adj.* 寒冷的
    scared (skɛrd) *adj.* 害怕的　　shake (ʃek) *v.* 發抖

Look at the picture for question 6.

6. (**A**) Who is feeding whom?

    A. A mother is giving her daughter food.

    B. They are a mother and a daughter.

    C. It is special baby food.

* feed〔fid〕v. 餵食（三態變化為：feed-fed-fed）
whom〔hum〕pron. 誰（who 的受格）
give〔gɪv〕v. 給   daughter〔'dɔtɚ〕n. 女兒
food〔fud〕n. 食物   special〔'spɛʃəl〕adj. 特別的
baby food 嬰兒食品

Look at the picture for question 7.

7. (**A**) What did the kitty do?

    A. It dirtied the bed.

    B. It is licking its leg.

    C. It is walking.

* kitty〔'kɪtɪ〕n. 小貓   dirty〔'dɝtɪ〕v. 弄髒
lick〔lɪk〕v. 舔   its〔ɪts〕pron. 牠的（it 的所有格）
leg〔lɛg〕n. 腿

Look at the picture for question 8.

8. (**B**) Why are her eyes shining?

    A. It's over $7,000 dollars.

    B. There is a special sale.

    C. The price is touching her.

* shine〔ʃaɪn〕v. 發出光芒
over〔'ovɚ〕prep. 超過（= *more than*）
special〔'spɛʃəl〕adj. 特別的   sale〔sel〕n. 拍賣
price〔praɪs〕n. 價格   touch〔tʌtʃ〕v. 觸動；感動

Look at the picture for question 9.

9. (**B**) Where is the food?

    A. It's for the dog.   B. It's in her hands.

    C. He cannot wait to eat.

    * *in her hands* 在她手上   *cannot wait to V.* 等不及要~

Look at the picture for question 10.

10. (**C**) What room is she in?

    A. It's a microwave oven.

    B. She is baking cookies.   C. It's the kitchen.

    * microwave (ˈmaɪkrəˌwev) *adj.* 微波的
    oven (ˈʌvən) *n.* 烤箱   *microwave oven* 微波爐
    bake (bek) *v.* 烘焙   cookie (ˈkʊkɪ) *n.* 餅乾
    kitchen (ˈkɪtʃɪn) *n.* 廚房

第二部份

11. (**B**) Will you lend me a pen?

    A. Yes, you may lend it.

    B. Sorry, but this is my only one.

    C. What color is it?

    * lend (lɛnd) *v.* 借 (出)   may (me) *aux.* 可以
    color (ˈkʌlɚ) *n.* 顏色

12. (**C**) Whose wedding did you attend?

    A. I will marry next year.

    B. It was at 2:00.   C. My brother's.

* whose〔huz〕*adj.* 誰的　　wedding〔'wɛdɪŋ〕*n.* 婚禮
attend〔ə'tɛnd〕*v.* 參加　　marry〔'mærɪ〕*v.* 結婚
next year 明年

13. (**C**)　How much did the thief get?

　　A.　Through the window.

　　B.　There were two of them.

　　C.　About fifty thousand.

　　* thief〔θif〕*n.* 小偷　　get〔gɛt〕*v.* 得到
　　　through〔θru〕*prep.* 穿過
　　　window〔'wɪndo〕*n.* 窗戶
　　　There were two of them. 他們有兩個人。
　　　fifty thousand 五萬

14. (**A**)　Is there anyone on the street?

　　A.　No, not a soul.

　　B.　Yes, it's raining.

　　C.　Go two blocks and turn left.

　　* street〔strit〕*n.* 街道　　soul〔sol〕*n.* 靈魂；人
　　　block〔blɑk〕*n.* 街區　　turn〔tɜn〕*v.* 轉向
　　　left〔lɛft〕*adv.* 向左邊

15. (**A**)　How many people can go on the tour bus?

　　A.　The maximum number of passengers is 18.

　　B.　We have a special price for large groups.

　　C.　It will leave when full.

* tour〔tʊr〕*n.* 旅行　　***tour bus*** 遊覽車
　maximum〔'mæksəməm〕*adj.* 最大的；最高的
　number〔'nʌmbɚ〕*n.* 人數
　passenger〔'pæsn̩dʒɚ〕*n.* 乘客
　special〔'spɛʃəl〕*adj.* 特別的　　price〔praɪs〕*n.* 價格
　large〔lɑrdʒ〕*adj.* 大的；多的　　group〔grup〕*n.* 團體
　leave〔liv〕*v.* 離開　　full〔fʊl〕*adj.* 滿的

16. (**A**)　Do you hear thunder?
　　　A.　Yes, a storm is coming.
　　　B.　No, I haven't heard from her.
　　　C.　No, I don't care for it.

　　　* hear〔hɪr〕*v.* 聽見　　thunder〔'θʌndɚ〕*n.* 雷；打雷
　　　　storm〔stɔrm〕*n.* 暴風雨
　　　　hear from 得到…的消息　　***care for*** 想要；喜歡

17. (**C**)　What a lovely scarf!
　　　A.　It's my favorite song, too.
　　　B.　It's delicious.　　　C.　Thank you. It's new.

　　　* lovely〔'lʌvlɪ〕*adj.* 可愛的；美麗的
　　　　scarf〔skɑrf〕*n.* 圍巾　　favorite〔'fevərɪt〕*adj.* 最喜愛的
　　　　song〔sɔŋ〕*n.* 歌曲　　delicious〔dɪ'lɪʃəs〕*adj.* 美味的

18. (**B**)　What's the population of your city?
　　　A.　Most people like to go shopping.
　　　B.　About one million.
　　　C.　Yes, we have many visitors.

* population〔,pɑpjə'leʃən〕*n.* 人口　　city〔'sɪtɪ〕*n.* 城市
go shopping 去購物　　million〔'mɪljən〕*n.* 百萬
visitor〔'vɪzɪtə〕*n.* 觀光客

19. (**B**) How many musicians are in the band?
    A. They play popular music.
    B. There are four.　　C. There is a piano in it.

    * musician〔mju'zɪʃən〕*n.* 音樂家　　band〔bænd〕*n.* 樂隊
    play〔ple〕*v.* 彈；演奏
    popular〔'pɑpjələ〕*adj.* 受歡迎的
    piano〔pɪ'æno〕*n.* 鋼琴

20. (**A**) Did you receive an invitation to Debra's party?
    A. Yes, I can't wait to go.
    B. Yes, I'll pay it right away.
    C. No, I haven't made a reservation.

    * receive〔rɪ'siv〕*v.* 接到；收到
    invitation〔,ɪnvə'teʃən〕*n.* 邀請函
    party〔'pɑrtɪ〕*n.* 派對
    I can't wait to go. 我等不及要去。
    pay〔pe〕*v.* 付錢　　**right away** 馬上；立刻
    reservation〔,rɛzə'veʃən〕*n.* 預訂

第三部份

21. (**C**) W: Did you have a PE class today?
    M: Yes, and it was very hard.
    W: What do you mean?
    M: Our teacher made us run two kilometers.

Question：How does the man probably feel?

A. Worried about the test.
B. Excited about the PE class.
C. Physically tired.

* PE〔'pi'i〕n. 體育（= physical education）
  hard〔hɑrd〕adj. 困難的；辛苦的
  mean〔min〕v. 意思是　　make〔mek〕v. 使…（做～）
  run〔rʌn〕v. 跑（三態變化為：run-ran-run）
  kilometer〔'kɪlə,mitɚ〕n. 公里
  probably〔'prɑbəblɪ〕adv. 可能
  feel〔fil〕v. 覺得　　worry〔'wɝɪ〕v. 擔心
  test〔tɛst〕n. 考試　　excited〔ɪk'saɪtɪd〕adj. 興奮的
  physically〔'fɪzɪkḷɪ〕adv. 在身體上
  tired〔taɪrd〕adj. 疲倦的

22.（ **B** ）M：Is your brother a university student?
　　　　　W：Yes, but he will graduate this year.
　　　　　M：What is he studying?
　　　　　W：He's a law student.

Question：What job will the woman's brother have?

A. He is a student.
B. He will be a lawyer.
C. He will have a graduation.

* university〔,junə'vɝsətɪ〕n. 大學
  graduate〔'grædʒʊ,et〕v. 畢業　　*this year* 今年
  law〔lɔ〕n. 法律　　*a law student* 法科學生
  job〔dʒɑb〕n. 工作；職業　　lawyer〔'lɔjɚ〕n. 律師
  graduation〔,grædʒʊ'eʃən〕n. 畢業

23. (**B**)　M：To the airport, please, and quickly.

　　　　W：Do you want the domestic or international terminal?

　　　　M：I'm going to Japan.　My plane leaves in one hour.

　　　Question：Where will the man go?

　　　A. In one hour.
　　　B. Japan.
　　　C. Quickly.

　　　* airport〔'ɛr͵port〕 *n.* 機場
　　　　quickly〔'kwɪklɪ〕 *adv.* 快地
　　　　domestic〔də'mɛstɪk〕 *adj.* 國內的
　　　　international〔͵ɪntɚ'næʃənḷ〕 *adj.* 國際的
　　　　terminal〔'tɝmənḷ〕 *n.*（機場的）航空站
　　　　Japan〔dʒə'pæn〕 *n.* 日本　　plane〔plen〕 *n.* 飛機
　　　　leave〔liv〕 *v.* 離開；出發　　*in one hour* 再過一小時

24. (**B**)　W：What did you have for breakfast today?

　　　　M：Cereal.　How about you?

　　　　W：I was too nervous to eat.

　　　Question：What does the woman mean?

　　　A. She ate cereal, too.
　　　B. She did not eat breakfast.
　　　C. She eats when she is nervous.

　　　* have〔hæv〕 *v.* 吃；喝　　breakfast〔'brɛkfəst〕 *n.* 早餐
　　　　cereal〔'sɪrɪəl〕 *n.* 穀物早餐　　*How about you?* 你呢 ?
　　　　too…to~ 太…以致不能~
　　　　nervous〔'nɝvəs〕 *adj.* 緊張的

25.(**B**) M: Where are the children?

W: They're on the playground.

M: I can't see them.

W: There they are, on the seesaw.

Question: What are the children doing?

A. They are missing.

B. They are playing together.

C. They are looking for their parents.

* playground ('ple,graund) *n.* 遊樂場；操場

There they are. 他們在那裡。

seesaw ('si,sɔ) *n.* 翹翹板

missing ('mɪsɪŋ) *adj.* 失蹤的；找不到的

together (tə'gɛðə) *adv.* 一起　　***look for*** 尋找

26.(**A**) W: Are those your new roller skates?

M: Yes, I got them yesterday.

W: So how do you like them?

M: I haven't tried them yet, but I can't wait.

Question: How does the man feel about the skates?

A. He is excited about them.

B. He does not know how to skate yet.

C. He doesn't like them very much.

* ***roller skates*** 溜冰輪鞋 (= *skates*)

get (gɛt) *v.* 買；得到

so (so) *adv.* 那麼；喔 (置於句首當感嘆詞用)

How do you like them? 你覺得它們如何；你喜歡它們嗎？

try (traɪ) *v.* 嘗試　　yet (jɛt) *adv.* 尚 (未) (用於否定句)

excited (ɪk'saɪtɪd) *adj.* 興奮的　　skate (sket) *v.* 溜冰

27. (**C**)   W: Would you like some tea?

          M: I don't want to trouble you.

          W: It's no trouble. I've already put the kettle on.

          Question: What does the woman mean?

          A. The man must drink more tea.

          B. It was a lot of trouble to find the kettle.

          C. She has already started to make tea.

      * ***Would you like~?*** 你要不要~?

        trouble (ˈtrʌbḷ) v. n. 麻煩

        already (ɔlˈrɛdɪ) adv. 已經　　　put (pʊt) v. 放

        kettle (ˈkɛtḷ) n. 茶壺　　must (mʌst) aux. 必須

        drink (drɪŋk) v. 喝

        It is a lot of trouble to V. ~是很麻煩的。

        find (faɪnd) v. 找到　　start (stɑrt) v. 開始

        make tea 沏茶;泡茶

28. (**A**)   M: Who was at the party last night?

          W: Most of my family were there.

          M: Even your niece?

          W: No, she is too young to stay up so late.

          Question: Who was probably at the party?

          A. The woman's sister.

          B. The man.

          C. The woman's niece.

      * ***most of~*** 大部分的~　　family (ˈfæməlɪ) n. 家人

        even (ˈivən) adv. 甚至　　niece (nis) n. 姪女;外甥女

        stay up 熬夜　　so (so) adv. 如此地

        late (let) adv. 晚

29. (**A**) M：Is this your hometown?

W：Oh, no. I'm from a village south of here.

M：So how do you like city life?

W：It's interesting but tiring.

Question：What does the man want to know?

A. Whether or not the woman likes big cities.

B. Whether or not the woman likes living in the north.

C. Whether or not the woman's village is interesting.

* hometown〔'hom,taun〕*n.* 家鄉

Oh, no. 噢，不是的。　　village〔'vɪlɪdʒ〕*n.* 村莊

south〔sauθ〕*n.* 南方　　**south of…** …的南方

city〔'sɪtɪ〕*n.* 城市　　life〔laɪf〕*n.* 生活

interesting〔'ɪntrɪstɪŋ〕*adj.* 有趣的

tiring〔'taɪrɪŋ〕*adj.* 令人厭倦的

whether〔'hwɛðɚ〕*conj.* 是否　　**whether or not** 是否～

live〔lɪv〕*v.* 住；生活　　north〔nɔrθ〕*n.* 北方

30. (**B**) W：Look. There's a rope in front of the painting.

M：That's so people can't get too close.

W：Why?

M：It must be worth a lot of money.

Question：Why is there a rope in front of the painting?

A. It is worthless.

B. It is valuable.

C. It is closed.

　　* rope〔rop〕n. 繩子　　***in front of***… 在…前面

　　　painting〔'pentɪŋ〕n. 畫

　　　That's so people can't get too close.

　　　(= ***That's the reason why people can't get too close.***)

　　　　如此一來，人們就不能靠得太近了。

　　　get〔gɛt〕v. 成為…狀態

　　　close〔klos〕adj. 接近的　　v.〔kloz〕關閉

　　　worth〔wɜθ〕adj. 有…價值的

　　　worthless〔'wɜθlɪs〕adj. 無價值的

　　　valuable〔'væljəbḷ〕adj. 珍貴的

二、閱讀能力測驗

第一部份：詞彙和結構

1. (**C**) Use the zebra crossing, <u>or</u> you will be hit by a car.

　　　走斑馬線，<u>否則</u>你會被車子撞到。

　　　　連接詞 or 引導的子句，若接在祈使句後，則作「否則」
　　　解，故依句意應選(C)。而 (A) and「就會…」，(B)
　　　when「何時」，(D) for「因為」，皆不合句意。

　　　* ***zebra crossing*** 斑馬線　　hit〔hɪt〕v. 撞到

2. (**D**) My father had a <u>mechanic</u> repair our car.

　　　我爸爸請<u>技工</u>修理我們的車。

　　　　(A) dentist〔'dɛntɪst〕n. 牙醫

　　　　(B) journalist〔'dʒɜnḷɪst〕n. 記者

　　　　(C) vendor〔'vɛndɚ〕n. 小販

　　　　(D) ***mechanic***〔mə'kænɪk〕n. 技工

　　　* have〔hæv〕v. 使（人）做…　　repair〔rɪ'pɛr〕v. 修理

3. (**A**) Greg ignored the red light and was fined NT$1200.

格瑞格不理會紅燈，被罰了台幣一千二百元。

(A) *ignore* (ɪgˋnor) v. 勿視；不理會

(B) illegal (ɪˋligḷ) adj. 犯法的

(C) past (pæst) prep. 經過

(D) drive (draɪv) v. 開車

* *red light* 紅燈　　fine (faɪn) v. 處以罰金

4. (**B**) You have to paste a stamp on the envelope before you mail it.

在你把它寄出去之前，你必須黏郵票在信封上。

(A) past (pæst) prep. 經過

(B) *paste* (pest) v. 黏貼

(C) post (post) v. 郵寄；張貼

(D) pack (pæk) v. 包裝

* stamp (stæmp) n. 郵票
envelope (ˋɛnvəˌlop) n. 信封
mail (mel) v. 郵寄

5. (**B**) If my pronunciation is wrong, please correct me.

如果我的發音不正確，請糾正我。

(A) connect (kəˋnɛkt) v. 連結

(B) *correct* (kəˋrɛkt) v. 指正；糾正

(C) check (tʃɛk) v. 檢查

(D) concern (kənˋsɝn) v. 使擔心

* pronunciation (prəˌnʌnsɪˋeʃən) n. 發音
wrong (rɔŋ) adj. 錯誤的

6. (**B**) He <u>had better</u> show up on time, or he will be fired.

他<u>最好</u>準時出現，否則會被解雇。

> ***had better***「最好」不論主詞是第幾人稱，一律用"***had***"
> ***better***，且後面一律接原形動詞，故選 (B)。

* ***show up*** 出現　　***on time*** 準時
fire〔faɪr〕*v.* 解雇

7. (**D**) Tim　　　： <u>How often</u> do you have your car washed?

Duncan：Once a week.

提姆：你<u>多久</u>把車送洗<u>一次</u>？

鄧肯：一星期一次。

(A) how far　多遠
(B) how soon　多快
(C) how long　多久；多長
(D) ***how often***　多久一次

* have〔hæv〕*v.* 使（人）做…　　wash〔wɑʃ〕*v.* 洗
once〔wʌns〕*adv.* 一次

8. (**D**) She <u>has been talking</u> on the phone for two hours.　Who is she talking to?

她<u>已經講了</u>兩個小時的電話了。她在跟誰說話？

> 從時間副詞 for two hours 及第二句得知，這動作由過去
> 某時開始，一直繼續到現在，仍在進行中，故須用「現在
> 完成進行式」，選 (D)。

* ***talk on the phone*** 講電話

9. (**A**) Could you <u>lend</u> me some money?　I lost my wallet.
你可以<u>借</u>我一些錢嗎？我的皮夾不見了。

$\begin{cases} \text{A lend B } sth. = \text{A lend } sth. \text{ to B}　\text{A 借給 B 某物 (A 借出)} \\ \text{A borrow } sth. \text{ from B}　\text{A 向 B 借某物 (B 借出)} \end{cases}$

依題意，借出者應為 "you"，故選(A) ***lend*** 〔 lɛnd 〕 v. 借
（出）。若用(C) borrow 〔ˊbaro 〕 v. 借（入），這句話應
改為 Can I borrow some money from you?　主詞要改
為 "I"。

* lose 〔 luz 〕 v. 遺失（三態變化為：lose-lost-lost）
wallet 〔ˊwɑlɪt 〕 n. 皮夾

10. (**A**) This pen is different <u>from</u> the one I lent you yesterday.
這枝筆和我昨天借你的那枝不同。

要表「與～不同」時，要用 be different from～，故選 (A)。

* different 〔ˊdɪfərənt 〕 adj. 不同的

11. (**B**) <u>As soon as</u> he saw the police, he started to run away.
他<u>一</u>看到警察，<u>就</u>開始逃。

(A) as long as　只要
(B) ***as soon as***　一…就～
(C) as fast as　像…一樣快
(D) as well as　以及

* police 〔 pəˊlis 〕 n. 警方　　start 〔 stɑrt 〕 v. 開始
run away 逃走

12. (**D**) Do you see that man <u>whose</u> coat is red?

你有看到那個外套是紅色的人嗎？

先行詞 that man 為人，故關係代名詞可用 who 或 that，
但由空格後的名詞（coat）知，應用具有形容詞性質的關
係代名詞的所有格 whose，以修飾其後的名詞，故選(D)。

* coat〔kot〕*n.* 外套

13. (**A**) It <u>took</u> me four hours to write this report.

寫這篇報告<u>花了</u>我四個小時。

$\begin{cases} 人 + spend + 時間 + (in) \text{ V-ing} \\ It + take \text{ (+ 人) } + 時間 + to \text{ V.} \end{cases}$

這題的主詞是 It，故應選 (A)。而 (C) use〔juz〕*v.* 使用，
(D) cost〔kɔst〕*v.* 花費（錢），均不合。

* report〔rɪ'port〕*n.* 報告

14. (**A**) It's impolite <u>of</u> Kate to say dirty words to the teacher.

凱特對老師說髒話，很沒禮貌。

It 是虛主詞，真正的主詞是後面的不定詞片語，而不定詞
意義上的主詞，則應在形容詞 impolite 後加 of，再接該
主詞，故選(A)。這類句型中的形容詞必須是對他人的稱
讚（如：kind, polite, wise）或責備（如：stupid,
impolite）。

* impolite〔,ɪmpə'laɪt〕*adj.* 無禮的
dirty〔'dɝtɪ〕*adj.* 髒的

15. (**C**) Jack heard Spot <u>scolded</u> by his master last night.

傑克昨晚聽到點點被他的主人罵。

hear（聽見）為感官動詞，而「點點<u>被</u>主人罵」，故受詞
補語應用「過去分詞」來表被動，故選 (C)。

* hear〔hɪr〕v. 聽見（三態變化為：hear-heard〔hɜd〕-heard）
spot〔spɑt〕n. 斑點（美國人喜歡將斑點狗取名 Spot）
master〔'mæstɚ〕n. 主人

第二部份：段落填空

Questions 16-21

It was getting dark. Some children and two Canadian
women were still <u>skating</u> on the ice. Suddenly the ice broke.
　　　　　　　　　16
One of the boys fell into the water. The children shouted,
"Help!" They didn't know <u>what</u> to do.
　　　　　　　　　　　　　17

天色變得越來越暗，但仍有些小孩和兩個加拿大女生在冰上溜冰。
突然間，冰破了，其中一個小男孩掉入水裡。孩子們大喊「救命！」他
們不知道該怎麼辦。

get〔gɛt〕v. 變得　　dark〔dɑrk〕adj. 暗的
Canadian〔kə'nedɪən〕adj. 加拿大的　n. 加拿大人
still〔stɪl〕adv. 仍然　　suddenly〔'sʌdn̩lɪ〕adv. 突然地
break〔brek〕v. 破裂　***fall into*** 掉入
shout〔ʃaut〕v. 大叫

16. (**B**) (A) boat〔bot〕v. 划船   (B) **skate**〔sket〕v. 溜冰
            (C) plant〔plænt〕v. 種植   (D) swim〔swɪm〕v. 游泳

17. (**C**) 疑問代名詞之後接不定詞，會形成「名詞片語」，四個選項均
            為疑問代名詞，但若選 (A) who 或 (B) when，do 的後面須
            接受詞；若選 (D)，則形成 where to do，不合理；故選 (C)
            what，形成 what to do 的名詞片語，當 know 的受詞。

The two Canadian friends heard them and skated <u>over</u> to get
                                                       18
the boy out of the water. The ice was <u>thin</u>. The two Canadians
                                          19
fell into the water, too. But they tried their best to save the little

boy. They knew they must be <u>quick</u>, or the boy would soon die.
                                20
Many people ran over to help. A young man jumped into the

water to save the three people. The boy and the two Canadian

women were out of the water <u>at last</u>.
                              21

　　那兩個加拿大籍的朋友聽到他們在呼救，所以就溜過去要把小男孩
救出水裡。冰很薄，這兩個加拿大人也掉入水裡，但是她們仍然盡力試
著要救那個小男孩。她們知道她們必須要快，否則小男孩很快就會死
掉。許多人都跑過來幫忙，有個年輕人跳入水裡，去救那三個人。那男
孩和兩個加拿大人，終於離開了水中。

        hear〔hɪr〕v. 聽見   **try one's best** 盡力
        save〔sev〕v. 救   or〔ɔr〕conj. 否則
        soon〔sun〕adv. 很快地   die〔daɪ〕v. 死亡
        jump〔dʒʌmp〕v. 跳

18. (**B**)　(A) ahead〔ə'hɛd〕*adv.* 在前面

　　　　　(B) *over*〔'ovɚ〕*adv.* 向那邊

　　　　　(C) by〔baɪ〕*adv.* 由旁邊經過

　　　　　(D) up〔ʌp〕*adv.* 向某場所接近（後面須接場所名稱）

19. (**D**)　(A) big〔bɪg〕*adj.* 大的　　(B) small〔smɔl〕*adj.* 小的

　　　　　(C) thick〔θɪk〕*adj.* 厚的　　(D) *thin*〔θɪn〕*adj.* 薄的

20. (**B**)　(A) slow〔slo〕*adj.* 慢的

　　　　　(B) *quick*〔kwɪk〕*adj.* 快的

　　　　　(C) sorry〔'sɔrɪ〕*adj.* 抱歉的

　　　　　(D) wrong〔rɔŋ〕*adj.* 錯誤的

21. (**D**)　(A) at all　一點也（不）　　(B) at least　至少

　　　　　(C) at first　起初　　　　　(D) *at last*　終於

Questions 22-25

Our house has two <u>stories</u>. It has three rooms on the second
　　　　　　　　　　22
floor. One is my brother's room, <u>another</u> is our study room, and
　　　　　　　　　　　　　　　　23
<u>the other</u> is mine. We <u>have lived</u> in this house for twelve years.
　24　　　　　　　　25
I was born and brought up in this house.

　　我們的房子有兩層樓，二樓有三個房間，一間是我哥哥的房間，一間是我們的書房，一間是我的房間。我們已經住在這房子十二年了，我在這個房子出生、長大。

　　　floor〔flor〕*n.* 樓層　　　*study room*　書房
　　　mine〔maɪn〕*pron.* 我的（東西）（在此表「我的房間」）
　　　be born 出生　　　*be brought up* 被撫養長大

22. (**C**)　(A) step〔stɛp〕*n.* 楷梯　　(B) stair〔stɛr〕*n.* 樓梯
　　　　　　(C) *story*〔'storɪ〕*n.* 樓層　(D) ceiling〔'silɪŋ〕*n.* 天花板

23. (**B**)　要分別說明前面提及的三個物件時，要用「one…,
　　　　　　another…, and the other….」，故在此應選 (B)。

24. (**D**)　要分別說明前面提及的三個物件時，要用「one…,
　　　　　　another…, and *the other*….」，故在此應選 (D)。

25. (**B**)　作者現在還住在這棟房子裡，所以是表「過去持續到現在的
　　　　　　狀態」，應用「現在完成式」，故選 (B)。「現在完成式」
　　　　　　常與 for, since 所引導的副詞連用，表持續之期間。

第三部份：閱讀理解

Questions 26-27

```
        甜蜜小舖

5/05/2006              下午 7:26
----------------------------------
數量        品名        價格
 1          襯衫        $390
 2          牛仔褲      $890／件
 1          皮帶        $450

總計                    $2,620
```

sweet〔swit〕*adj.* 甜蜜的
P.M.〔'pi'ɛm〕*adv.* 午後（= *p.m.*）
Qty. = quantity〔'kwɑntətɪ〕*n.* 數量
item〔'aɪtəm〕*n.* 項目　　price〔praɪs〕*n.* 價格
shirt〔ʃɜt〕*n.* 襯衫　　jeans〔dʒinz〕*n. pl.* 牛仔褲
belt〔bɛlt〕*n.* 皮帶　　total〔'totḷ〕*n.* 總計

26. (**D**) 這是一張甜蜜小舖的<u>收據</u>。

(A) notice〔'notɪs〕*n.* 告示　　(B) sign〔saɪn〕*n.* 標誌

(C) check〔tʃɛk〕*n.* 支票　　(D) *receipt*〔rɪ'sit〕*n.* 收據

27. (**A**) 哪一個品目可能可以在甜蜜小舖買到？

(A) *trousers*〔'traʊzɚz〕*n. pl.* 褲子

(B) carpet〔'kɑrpɪt〕*n.* 地毯

(C) glue〔glu〕*n.* 膠水

(D) robot〔'robət〕*n.* 機器人

* available〔ə'veləbḷ〕*adj.* 可買到的；可獲得的

Questions 28-30

吃對的食物

下面的金字塔告訴你，每天應該吃什麼種類的食物，會有益健康。

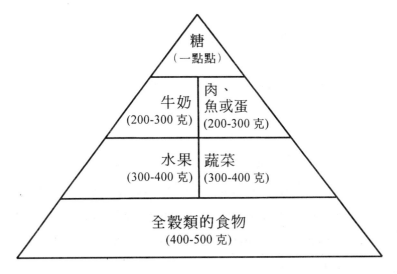

right〔raɪt〕adj. 正確的   kind〔kaɪnd〕n. 種類
pyramid〔'pɪrəmɪd〕n. 金字塔
below〔bə'lo〕adv. 在下方   show〔ʃo〕v. 顯示
healthy〔'hɛlθɪ〕adj. 有益健康的   sugar〔'ʃʊgɚ〕n. 糖
milk〔mɪlk〕n. 牛奶   meat〔mit〕n. 肉
vegetable〔'vɛdʒətəbl̩〕n. 蔬菜   whole〔hol〕adj. 所有的
grain〔gren〕n. 穀物   **whole-grain** adj. 全穀類的

28. (**C**) 我們每天應該吃最多的什麼？
     (A) 肉或魚。 (B) 蔬菜。 (C) 全穀類食物。 (D) 水果。

29. (**D**) 我們每天應該吃最少的什麼？
     (A) 牛奶。   (B) 水果。 (C) 肉或魚。   (D) 糖。
     * least〔list〕adv. 最少

30. (**A**) 哪一樣應該多吃，牛奶還是肉？
     (A) 一樣多的牛奶和肉。
     (B) 比牛奶少的肉。
     (C) 較多的牛奶，較少的肉。
     (D) 較多的肉，較少的牛奶。
     * **as much** A **as** B A 與 B 一樣多

Questions 31-33

Do you celebrate April Fools' Day? In many western countries, on this day, you may play a joke or a funny trick on another person. But your activity must be safe. You must only try to make that person feel foolish. Then you can laugh and yell out "April Fools'."

你有慶祝愚人節嗎？這一天，在許多西方國家，你可以開別人的玩笑，或捉弄別人。但是你的動作必須是安全的。你必須只是試著使那個人覺得愚蠢，然後你可以笑，並且大叫「愚人節快樂」。

celebrate〔ˈsɛlə,bret〕v. 慶祝　　April〔ˈeprəl〕n. 四月
fool〔ful〕n. 傻瓜　***April Fools' Day*** 愚人節
western〔ˈwɛstɚn〕adj. 西方的　　joke〔dʒok〕n. 笑話
play a joke on sb. 開某人的玩笑　　funny〔ˈfʌnɪ〕adj. 好玩的
trick〔trɪk〕n. 惡作劇　***play a trick on sb.*** 對某人惡作劇
another〔əˈnʌðɚ〕adj. 另一的　　activity〔ækˈtɪvətɪ〕n. 活動
safe〔sef〕adj. 安全的　　make〔mek〕v. 使
feel〔fil〕v. 覺得　　foolish〔ˈfulɪʃ〕adj. 愚蠢的
then〔ðɛn〕adv. 然後　　laugh〔læf〕v. 笑
yell〔jɛl〕v. 大聲說　***yell out*** 大叫

The history of April Fools' Day is not totally clear. Some believe it came from several different cultures, and their celebrations involving the first day of spring. Some say it started in France, while others believe it began in England or Scotland. No matter where it started, by the eighteenth century, April Fools' Day had become an international fun day.

愚人節的歷史由來並不是很清楚。有些人認為它來自好幾個不同的文化，以及與春天的第一天有關的慶祝活動。有些人說它始於法國，然而有些人則認為它開始於英格蘭或蘇格蘭。不管它是從哪裡開始的，到了十八世紀的時候，愚人節就已經變成一個國際性的趣味節日。

history (′hɪstrɪ) *n.* 歷史　　totally (′totḷɪ) *adv.* 全然；完全地

clear (klɪr) *adj.* 清楚的　　some (sʌm) *pron.* 有些人

believe (bɪ′liv) *v.* 相信；認為　　several (′sɛvərəl) *adj.* 幾個

culture (′kʌltʃə) *n.* 文化

celebration (ˌsɛlə′breʃən) *n.* 慶祝活動

involve (ɪn′valv) *v.* 與…有關　　spring (sprɪŋ) *n.* 春天

some…others ~　有些…有些~　　while (hwaɪl) *conj.*　然而

start (start) *v.* 開始　　begin (bɪ′gɪn) *v.* 開始

England (′ɪŋglənd) *n.* 英格蘭

Scotland (′skatlənd) *n.* 蘇格蘭

no matter where　不論什麼地方　　by (baɪ) *prep.* 在…之前

eighteenth (e′tinθ) *adj.*　第十八的

century (′sɛntʃərɪ) *n.* 世紀　　become (bɪ′kʌm) *v.* 變成

international (ˌɪntə′næʃənḷ) *adj.*　國際性的

fun (fʌn) *adj.* 有趣的

In early America, one popular trick was to stick a funny note like, "Kick me" or "I'm stupid" on someone's back without them knowing it! Would you ever do that?

　　在早期的美國，有一個很受歡迎的惡作劇，就是在別人不知情的情況下，在他們背後貼上有趣的紙條，像是「踢我」或「我是笨蛋」！你曾經這麼做過嗎？

early (′ɝlɪ) *adj.* 早期的　　America (ə′mɛrɪkə) *n.* 美國

popular (′papjələ) *adj.* 受歡迎的　　stick (stɪk) *v.* 貼

funny (′fʌnɪ) *adj.* 好笑的　　note (not) *n.* 字條

kick (kɪk) *v.* 踢　　stupid (′stjupɪd) *adj.* 笨的

back (bæk) *n.* 背　　without (wɪð′aʊt) *prep.* 沒有

ever (′ɛvə) *adv.* 曾經

31. (**B**) 關於愚人節，什麼是重要的事？

(A) 你的惡作劇必須要很好笑。

(B) 你的惡作劇不能造成傷害。

(C) 你不可以說謊。

(D) 你不可以嘲笑別人。

* cause〔kɔz〕v. 造成　　harm〔hɑrm〕n. 傷害
lie〔laɪ〕v. 說謊　　**make fun of sb.** 嘲笑某人

32. (**D**) 這個節日可能是從世界的哪個地方開始的？

(A) 亞洲。　　　　　　(B) 北美洲。

(C) 中東。　　　　　　(D) 歐洲。

* probably〔'prɑbəblɪ〕adv. 可能
Asia〔'eʃə〕n. 亞洲　　north〔nɔrθ〕adj. 北方的
North America 北美洲　　middle〔'mɪdḷ〕adj. 中間的
east〔ist〕n. 東方　　**the Middle East** 中東
Europe〔'jurəp〕n. 歐洲

33. (**C**) 愚人節是一個_____的機會。

(A) 生火　　　　　　(B) 叫別人白痴

(C) 做一些幽默的事　　(D) 在陌生人面前裝傻

* chance〔tʃæns〕n. 機會　　fire〔faɪr〕n. 火
start a fire 升火　　call〔kɔl〕v. 叫
idiot〔'ɪdɪət〕n. 笨蛋；白痴
humorous〔'hjumərəs〕adj. 幽默的
silly〔'sɪlɪ〕adj. 愚蠢的　　**in front of** 在…面前
stranger〔'strendʒɚ〕n. 陌生人

Questions 34-35

威廉英語學院

◎ 英語課程
◎ 小班制 （每班 12 個學生）
◎ 招收 480 個學生
◎ 八週的課程

詳情請洽：
   校長
   威廉英語學院
   倫敦市蘋果街 38 號
   電話：01-123-4567

---

institute〔'ɪnstə,tjut〕*n.* 學院   course〔kors〕*n.* 課程
class〔klæs〕*n.* 班   further〔'fɝðɚ〕*adj.* 更進一步的
information〔,ɪnfɚ'meʃən〕*n.* 訊息
contact〔'kɑntækt〕*n.* 接洽；聯繫
headmaster〔'hɛd'mæstɚ〕*n.* 校長
London〔'lʌndən〕*n.* 倫敦

34. (**C**) 這個學院位於_____。
   (A) America〔ə'mɛrɪkə〕*n.* 美國（= *the U.S.A.* ）
   (B) Australia〔ɔ'streljə〕*n.* 澳洲
   (C) *England*〔'ɪŋglənd〕*n.* 英國
   (D) Canada〔'kænədə〕*n.* 加拿大

35. (**A**) 這個學院想要得到什麼人？
   (A) 學生。   (B) 老師。   (C) 工人。   (D) 醫生。
   * have〔hæv〕*v.* 得到

全民英語能力分級檢定測驗
初級測驗③

一、聽力測驗

　　本測驗分三部份，全爲三選一之選擇題，每部份各 10 題，共 30 題，作答時間約 20 分鐘。

第一部份：看圖辨義

　　　　本部份共 10 題，試題冊上每題有一個圖片，請聽錄音機播出一個相關的問題，與 A、B、C 三個英語敘述後，選一個與所看到圖片最相符的答案，並在答案紙上相對的圓圈內塗黑作答。每題播出一遍，問題及選項均不印在試題冊上。

例：（看）

NT$80　　NT$50

　　　　　（聽）

　　　　　Look at the picture.　How much is the hamburger?

　　　　　　A.　It's eighty dollars.
　　　　　　B.　It's fifty-five dollars.
　　　　　　C.　It's eighteen dollars.

　　　　　正確答案爲 A

Question 1

Question 2

Question 3

MENU

Soup		Desserts	
onion soup	$60	cheesecake	$50
beef soup	$80	ice cream	$55
salads		**Drinks**	
tomato salad	$50	orange juice	$80
green salad	$70	black tea	$70

Question 4

Question 5

請 翻 頁 ⟹

Question 6

Question 7

Question 8

Question 9

Question 10

Chris's Schedule

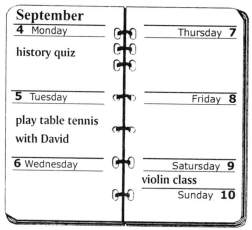

請翻頁 ▮⟹

第二部份：問答

本部份共 10 題，每題錄音機會播出一個問句或直述句，每題播出一次，聽後請從試題冊上 A、B、C 三個選項中，選出一個最適合的回答或回應，並在答案紙上塗黑作答。

例：

（聽） Good morning, Kevin. How are you?

（看） A. I'm fine, thank you.
B. I'm in the living room.
C. My name is Kevin.

正確答案為 A

11. A. Sure. There are lots of channels to choose from.
B. Yes, I'd love to.
C. No, it's not broken.

12. A. Over 2000 work here.
B. Only 30 people applied for the job.
C. It pays its people well.

13. A. It took about an hour and a half.
B. No, I was speeding.
C. I got a flat tire.

14. A. It came today.
B. Yes, I just posted it.
C. I've almost finished it.

15. A. I'd prefer to play
       basketball.
    B. No, I don't know how
       to play.
    C. At least four.

16. A. It cost 500 dollars.
    B. Thank you. I like it,
       too.
    C. I'd like a haircut,
       please.

17. A. No. It's raining.
    B. No, the car is on the
       street.
    C. No, it's not near the
       park.

18. A. I like them, too.
    B. That will be 50
       dollars.
    C. No, thanks. I don't
       want any.

19. A. From ten until six.
    B. At ten-thirty.
    C. On September first.

20. A. They're on your
       head.
    B. No, it was sold out.
    C. Look in the closet.

請 翻 頁

第三部份： 簡短對話

本部份共 10 題，每題錄音機會播出一段對話及一個相關的問題，每題播出兩次，聽後請從試題冊上 A、B、C 三個選項中，選出一個最適合的回答，並在答案紙上塗黑作答。

例：

(聽) (Woman) Good afternoon, …Mr. Davis?

(Man) Yes. I have an appointment with Dr. Sanders at two o'clock. My son Tommy has a fever.

(Woman) Oh, that's too bad. Well, please have a seat, Mr. Davis. Dr. Sanders will be right with you.

Question: Where did this conversation take place?

(看) A. In a post office.

B. In a restaurant.

C. In a doctor's office.

正確答案為 C

21. A. During the 1900s.
    B. For 100 years.
    C. He will come next week.

22. A. She lost the old ones.
    B. She lost her contact lenses.
    C. We do not know.

23. A. She works in other people's houses.
    B. She is employed by a company.
    C. She is a housewife.

24. A. His swimming suit.
    B. A jacket and tie.
    C. Informal clothes.

25. A. Yes, he will use his credit card to buy something.
    B. No, he does not have enough money.
    C. Yes, but he will buy it later.

請 翻 頁 ⁝⟹

26. A. She likes it.
    B. She has no other way to get to work.
    C. Her scooter is not working.

27. A. Stop wasting money.
    B. Stop buying the newspaper.
    C. Recycle her trash.

28. A. It is going to rain.
    B. She might get bitten.
    C. She might get cold.

29. A. How to find the word in the dictionary.
    B. How to write the word.
    C. How to say the word.

30. A. Seven days.
    B. Only a few days.
    C. More than two weeks.

二、閱讀能力測驗

本測驗分三部份，全為四選一之選擇題，共 35 題，作答時間 35 分鐘。

第一部份： 詞彙和結構

本部份共15題，每題含一個空格。請就試題冊上A、B、C、D四個選項中選出最適合題意的字或詞，標示在答案紙上。

1. _____ drink do you like the most?
   A. What kind of
   B. What a kind of
   C. What kind
   D. What a kind of a

2. I have so _____ time to prepare for the final exam.
   A. few
   B. little
   C. a few
   D. a little

3. Joan is the most skillful hairdresser _____ I have ever seen.
   A. which
   B. who
   C. whom
   D. that

請 翻 頁 ⮕

4. Call an _____, please! Someone is hurt.
   A. alphabet
   B. ambulance
   C. accident
   D. actress

5. Give up smoking, or it will _____ your health.
   A. offer
   B. improve
   C. increase
   D. affect

6. I need shrimp. Could you go to the _____ and buy some for me?
   A. convenience store
   B. stationery store
   C. post office
   D. supermarket

7. Guava is a bit hard. _____ eat something softer?
   A. Why not
   B. Why not to
   C. Why don't
   D. Why you not

8. We will go mountain climbing if it _____ a clear day this Sunday.

   A. was

   B. will be

   C. is

   D. to be

9. _____ Jeff. Is Bruce there? I want to talk to him.

   A. There is

   B. This is

   C. He is

   D. Here is

10. Let's go for a walk, _____ we?

   A. shall

   B. will

   C. don't

   D. do

11. Chris : Do you like my new necktie?

   Jesse : Yes, very much. I'll buy _____ for my father.

   A. it

   B. a

   C. one

   D. the other

請 翻 頁

12. George is the thinnest of _____.

    A. us all

    B. all us

    C. we all

    D. all we

13. Danny was lucky _____ to win the lottery.

    A. much

    B. enough

    C. very

    D. a lot

14. Peter is a dishonest person. I don't trust him _____.

    A. after all

    B. in all

    C. at all

    D. for all

15. Will you _____ me a favor? I can't start my car.

    A. bring

    B. find

    C. make

    D. do

第二部份：段落填空
　　　　本部份共10題，包括二個段落，每個段落各含5個空格。請就試題冊上A、B、C、D四個選項中選出最適合題意的字或詞，標示在答案紙上。

Questions 16-19

Sam: This menu has a lot of good ___(16)___ . In fact, everything ___(17)___ delicious. I'm going to have the roast beef.

Tom: I've ___(18)___ a few pounds lately. I'm going to have fish and salad.

Sam: Tom, you're so thin. You don't have to ___(19)___ . Look at me! I'm the one who should eat fish and salad.

16. A. snack
    B. cooks
    C. dishes
    D. price

17. A. cooks
    B. checks
    C. chooses
    D. looks

18. A. won
    B. gained
    C. lifted
    D. raised

19. A. eat
    B. diet
    C. cook
    D. wash dishes

請翻頁 ⫸

Questions 20-25

Thomas Edison was a famous American inventor. When he was a child, he was always trying out new ___(20)___. Young Edison was ___(21)___ for only three months. During those three months he asked his teacher a lot of questions. Most of the questions were not about his lessons. His teacher thought he wasn't ___(22)___ and told his mother to take him out of school. Edison's mother had to teach him ___(23)___. Edison learnt very quickly. He read a lot. Later he became very interested in ___(24)___ and invented many ___(25)___ things.

20. A. answers
    B. ideas
    C. questions
    D. ways

21. A. at home
    B. on the farm
    C. in school
    D. by the river

22. A. kind
    B. clever
    C. bad
    D. forgetful

23. A. a lesson
    B. lonely
    C. himself
    D. herself

24. A. science
    B. art
    C. history
    D. music

25. A. terrible
    B. common
    C. chemical
    D. useful

第三部份： 閱讀理解

　　本部份共 10 題，包括數段短文，每段短文後有 1~3 個相關問題，請就試題冊上 A、B、C、D 四個選項中選出最適合者，標示在答案紙上。

Question 26

PLEASE KEEP OFF
THE GRASS

26. What does this sign mean?

A. Please plant more grass.

B. Keep the grass in a safe place.

C. Don't leave the grass.

D. Don't go on the grass.

請 翻 頁 ▐◁⟹

Questions 27-29

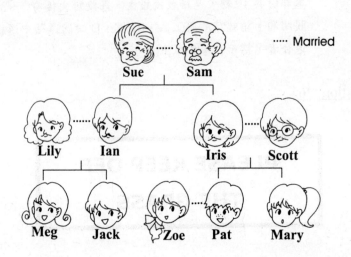

····· Married

27. Who is Mary's cousin?

    A. Lily.   B. Ian.

    C. Jack.   D. Zoe.

28. Who is Scott's niece?

    A. Lily.   B. Jack.

    C. Meg.   D. Ian.

29. Who is Mary's sister-in-law?

    A. Lily.   B. Meg.

    C. Zoe.   D. None.

Questions 30-32

JOB APPLICATION FORM

YOUR NAME : David Chen

ADDRESS : No. 123 Dai-Hsieh Rd., Hsinchiu

PHONE NUMBER : (03)222-3456

HIGH SCHOOL	Cheng Kung High School
KEY COURSE	computers, 3 years; maths, 4years; chemistry, 2 years
LANGUAGES	Japanese, 3 years (reading, writing, speaking); French, 2 years (reading, writing)
EXPERIENCE	Delivering newspapers; taking food orders at Smith's
INTERESTS	I like traveling and playing basketball. After school I often play basketball with my friends and I usually travel on my holidays. I enjoy working with people and helping them.

---

30. We can't find David Chen's _____ on the form.

 A. interests   B. address

 C. age   D. experience

請 翻 頁 ◖◀⟶

31. Where has he worked?
    A. In a restaurant.
    B. In a police station.
    C. In a post office.
    D. In a computer company.

32. What is David's favorite exercise?
    A. Computer.
    B. Traveling.
    C. Math.
    D. Basketball.

Questions 33-35

First invented in the 1940s, TV became very popular in the 1950s. By 1960, almost every U.S. living room had a TV. For over fifty years now, television has influenced the way we live.

Children are most affected by television. This worries many parents and teachers because most TV programs have no educational value. Cartoons and violent programs are entertaining, but have no benefits. The biggest worry of parents and teachers is that TV causes lower math and reading scores. Because of so much time spent watching TV, children are spending less time reading and thinking independently.

Kids in America watch more than two hours of TV a day on weekdays and over five hours a day on weekends. Experts say that if we all want to do better and be better, we must limit our TV watching.

33. Why are parents and teachers worried about TV?
    A. Because kids are becoming dangerous.
    B. Because crime is rising.
    C. Because test grades are getting lower.
    D. Because the cartoons are too boring.

34. When did most people in America have a television?
    A. Over a century ago.
    B. Over seventy years ago.
    C. In the 1950s.
    D. In the 1940s.

35. About how many hours of TV do U.S. kids watch in a week?
    A. Over forty hours.
    B. Around thirty hours.
    C. Fourteen hours.
    D. About twenty hours.

初級英檢模擬試題③詳解

一、聽力測驗

第一部份

Look at the picture for question 1.

1. (**C**) What is he listening to?
   A. He is going fast.
   B. He is skateboarding.
   C. Music from the radio.

   * ***listen to*** 傾聽　　fast〔fæst〕*adv.* 迅速地
   skateboard〔'sket,bord〕*v.* 溜滑板
   music〔'mjuzɪk〕*n.* 音樂　　radio〔'redɪ,o〕*n.* 收音機

Look at the picture for question 2.

2. (**A**) What is in the boy's hand?
   A. A small plant.　　B. On his face.
   C. She is rude.

   * plant〔plænt〕*n.* 植物　　face〔fes〕*n.* 臉
   rude〔rud〕*adj.* 無禮的

Look at the picture for question 3.

3. (**C**) How many items are there?
   A. Two drinks.　　B. Under $80.
   C. Eight things.

   * ***How many~?*** 有多少個~?　　item〔'aɪtəm〕*n.* 項目
   drink〔drɪŋk〕*n.* 飲料　　under〔'ʌndɚ〕*prep.* 低於…

Look at the picture for question 4.

4.(**B**) What is behind the boy?

A. He is drawing a face.　　B. There is a snowman.

C. The snow is falling.

* behind〔bɪˈhaɪnd〕 *prep.* 在…後面　　draw〔drɔ〕 *v.* 畫
snowman〔ˈsnoˌmæn〕 *n.* 雪人　　snow〔sno〕 *n.* 雪
fall〔fɔl〕 *v.* 下 (雪)

Look at the picture for question 5.

5.(**A**) Who is throwing the card?

A. The boy on the right.　　B. They are playing cards.

C. She's in the middle.

* throw〔θro〕 *v.* 丟　　card〔kard〕 *n.* 紙牌；卡片
right〔raɪt〕 *n.* 右邊　　*play cards* 玩紙牌
middle〔ˈmɪdl〕 *n.* 中間

Look at the picture for question 6.

6.(**C**) Are the girls enjoying the concert?

A. Because the singer is very handsome.

B. No, she is screaming.

C. Yes, they are having a lot of fun.

* enjoy〔ɪnˈdʒɔɪ〕 *v.* 喜歡；享受
concert〔ˈkansɝt〕 *n.* 音樂會；演唱會
singer〔ˈsɪŋɚ〕 *n.* 歌手
handsome〔ˈhænsəm〕 *adj.* 英俊的
scream〔skrim〕 *v.* 尖叫
have a lot of fun 玩得很愉快

Look at the picture for question 7.

7. (**B**) Why does the man feel upset?

    A. He doesn't know Jacky.

    B. There is no address on the envelope.

    C. He is a mailman.

    * feel〔fil〕v. 覺得　　upset〔ʌpˋsɛt〕adj. 心煩的
      know〔no〕v. 知道；認識
      address〔əˋdrɛs , ˋædrɛs〕n. 地址
      envelope〔ˋɛnvə,lop〕n. 信封
      mailman〔ˋmel,mæn〕n. 郵差

Look at the picture for question 8.

8. (**C**) What is the hen doing?

    A. It's chasing the chickens.

    B. They are running away.

    C. It's striking the cat.

    * hen〔hɛn〕n. 母雞　　chase〔tʃes〕v. 追逐
      chicken〔ˋtʃɪkən〕n. 雞　　*run away* 逃跑
      strike〔straɪk〕v. 打

Look at the picture for question 9.

9. (**B**) Who has the brush?

    A. The young girl.

    B. The lady who is standing.

    C. It hurts.

    * brush〔brʌʃ〕n. 梳子　　young〔jʌŋ〕adj. 年輕的
      stand〔stænd〕v. 站著　　hurt〔hɝt〕v. 疼痛

Look at the picture for question 10.

10. (**A**) When will Chris do exercise?

　　A. On September fifth.

　　B. On September fourth.

　　C. On September ninth.

　　* exercise (ˈɛksɚˌsaɪz) n. 運動
　　　September (sɛpˈtɛmbɚ) n. 九月
　　　fifth (fɪfθ) n. (每月的) 五日 (= 5ᵗʰ)
　　　fourth (forθ) n. (每月的) 四日 (= 4ᵗʰ)
　　　ninth (naɪnθ) n. (每月的) 九日 (= 9ᵗʰ)

第二部份

11. (**A**) Do you like to watch cable TV?

　　A. Sure. There are lots of channels to choose from.

　　B. Yes, I'd love to.　　C. No, it's not broken.

　　* cable (ˈkebḷ) n. 電纜　　*cable TV* 有線電視
　　　sure (ʃur) adv. 當然　　channel (ˈtʃænḷ) n. 頻道
　　　choose (tʃuz) v. 選擇　　broken (ˈbrokən) adj. 故障的

12. (**A**) How many people does the factory employ?

　　A. Over 2000 work here.

　　B. Only 30 people applied for the job.

　　C. It pays its people well.

　　* factory (ˈfæktrɪ) n. 工廠
　　　employ (ɪmˈplɔɪ) v. 雇用　　over (ˈovɚ) prep. 超過
　　　apply (əˈplaɪ) v. 申請；應徵 < for >
　　　pay (pe) v. 支付 (薪水)　　well (wɛl) adv. 好地

13. (**C**) Why did it take you so long to drive here?

    A. It took about an hour and a half.

    B. No, I was speeding.

    C. I got a flat tire.

    * take〔tek〕v. 花費（時間）　　long〔lɔŋ〕adj. 久的

       an hour and a half 一個半小時

       speed〔spid〕v. 超速行駛

       flat〔flæt〕adj. 平坦的　　tire〔taɪr〕n. 輪胎

       flat tire 洩了氣的輪胎

14. (**A**) Have you received the letter yet?

    A. It came today.

    B. Yes, I just posted it.

    C. I've almost finished it.

    * receive〔rɪ'siv〕v. 收到

       yet〔jɛt〕adv. 已經（用於疑問句）；尚（未）（用於否定句）

       just〔dʒʌst〕adv. 剛剛　　post〔post〕v. 郵寄

       almost（'ɔl,most）adv. 幾乎　　finish（'fɪnɪʃ）v. 完成

15. (**C**) How many players do we need for this game?

    A. I'd prefer to play basketball.

    B. No, I don't know how to play.

    C. At least four.

    * player（'pleɚ）n. 球員　　game〔gem〕n. 比賽

       prefer（prɪ'fɝ）v. 比較喜歡

       basketball（'bæskɪt,bɔl）n. 籃球

       at least 至少

16. (**A**) How much did the hairdresser charge you?

   A. It cost 500 dollars.

   B. Thank you. I like it, too.

   C. I'd like a haircut, please.

   * hairdresser〔'hɛr͵drɛsɚ〕 *n.* 美髮師
     charge〔tʃɑrdʒ〕 *v.* 收費；向 (某人) 索取 (費用)
     cost〔kɔst〕 *v.* 花費；值
     dollar〔'dɑlɚ〕 *n.* 元
     haircut〔'hɛr͵kʌt〕 *n.* 理髮

17. (**B**) Did you park in the garage?

   A. No. It's raining.

   B. No, the car is on the street.

   C. No, it's not near the park.

   * park〔pɑrk〕 *v.* 停車　 *n.* 公園
     garage〔gə'rɑʒ〕 *n.* 車庫
     near〔nɪr〕 *prep.* 在⋯附近

18. (**B**) I'd like two mangoes.

   A. I like them, too.

   B. That will be 50 dollars.

   C. No, thanks. I don't want any.

   * *I'd like* 我想要 (= *I want*)
     mango〔'mæŋgo〕 *n.* 芒果

19. (**B**) What time does the museum open?

   A. From ten until six.

   B. At ten-thirty.

   C. On September first.

   * museum〔mju'ziəm〕*n.* 博物館

    open〔'opən〕*v.* 開始營業；開門

    until〔ən'tɪl〕*prep.* 直到（= *till*）

    September〔sɛp'tɛmbɚ〕*n.* 九月（= *Sept.*）

20. (**C**) Have you seen my slippers?

   A. They're on your head.

   B. No, it was sold out.

   C. Look in the closet.

   * slippers〔'slɪpɚz〕*n. pl.* 拖鞋

    head〔hɛd〕*n.* 頭　　***sell out*** 售完

    look in 往…裡面看一下

    closet〔'klɑzɪt〕*n.* 櫃子；衣櫥

第三部份

21. (**A**) M：Have you heard of Picasso?

   W：Of course, he was one of the greatest artists of the

     last century.

   M：There will be a show of his paintings at the museum

     next week.

   W：Great!　Let's go.

Question：When did Picasso live?

A. During the 1900s.

B. For 100 years.

C. He will come next week.

* ***heard of*** 聽說過　Picasso〔pɪ'kɑso〕*n.* 畢卡索

   greatest〔'gretɪst〕*adj.* 最偉大的（great 的最高級）

   artist〔'ɑrtɪst〕*n.* 藝術家　last〔læst〕*adj.* 上一個

   century〔'sɛntʃərɪ〕*n.* 世紀

   show〔ʃo〕*n.* 展示會

   painting〔'pentɪŋ〕*n.* 畫　live〔lɪv〕*v.* 活

   during〔'djʊrɪŋ〕*prep.* 在…期間

   the 1900s 二十世紀

22. (**C**)　M：Did you get new glasses?

   W：Yes, I did.

   M：I thought you wanted contact lenses.

   W：I did, but my mother was afraid I would lose them.

   Question：Why did the woman get new glasses?

   A. She lost the old ones.

   B. She lost her contact lenses.

   C. We do not know.

   * get〔gɛt〕*v.* 買

      glasses〔'glæsɪz〕*n. pl.* 眼鏡

      think〔θɪŋk〕*v.* 以為（三態變化為：think-thought-thought）

      contact lenses 隱形眼鏡　lose〔luz〕*v.* 遺失

23. (**B**)　W: Who does the housework in your house?

M: We all help, but my mother does most of it.

W: Is she a housewife?

M: No, she also has a job.

Question: What does the man's mother do?

A. She works in other people's houses.

B. She is employed by a company.

C. She is a housewife.

* housework ('haʊs,wɜk) *n.* 家事

most (most) *pron.* 大部分

housewife ('haʊs,waɪf) *n.* 家庭主婦

job (dʒɑb) *n.* 工作；職業

What does *sb.* ***do?*** 某人的職業是什麼？

employ (ɪm'plɔɪ) *v.* 雇用

company ('kʌmpənɪ) *n.* 公司

24. (**B**)　M: Is the party formal?

W: Yes, it is.

M: What should I wear?

W: You should wear a suit.

Question: What will the man wear to the party?

A. His swimming suit.　　B. A jacket and tie.

C. Informal clothes.

* formal ('fɔrml̩) *adj.* 正式的　　wear (wɛr) *v.* 穿

suit (sut) *n.* 西裝　　***swimming suit*** 泳裝

jacket ('dʒækɪt) *n.* 夾克　　tie (taɪ) *n.* 領帶

informal (ɪn'fɔrml̩) *adj.* 不正式的

25. (**A**) W: That will be 1,200 dollars.

M: Oh, I don't think I have enough money.

W: We take all major credit cards.

M: All right. I'll charge it.

Question: Will the man buy anything?

A. Yes, he will use his credit card to buy something.

B. No, he does not have enough money.

C. Yes, but he will buy it later.

* enough〔ə'nʌf〕*adj.* 足夠的　　take〔tek〕*v.* 接受

major〔'medʒɚ〕*adj.* 主要的　***credit card*** 信用卡

All right. 好的。

charge〔tʃɑrdʒ〕*v.* 賒買；把消費記帳上

charge it 刷卡　　later〔'letɚ〕*adv.* 稍後；待會

26. (**A**) M: Do you have a scooter?

W: Yes, but I rarely ride it.

M: Why not?

W: I prefer to take the MRT to work.

Question: Why does the woman take the MRT to work?

A. She likes it.

B. She has no other way to get to work.

C. Her scooter is not working.

* scooter〔'skutɚ〕*n.* 輕型摩托車

rarely〔'rɛrlɪ〕*adv.* 很少　　ride〔raɪd〕*v.* 騎

prefer〔prɪ'fɝ〕*v.* 比較喜歡

take〔tek〕*v.* 搭乘（交通工具）

MRT 大眾捷運系統（= *Mass Rapid Transit*）

other〔'ʌðɚ〕*adj.* 其他的　　way〔we〕*n.* 方法

work〔wɝk〕*v.* 運作；運轉　***get to work*** 到達工作場所

27. (**C**) M：Where should I put this old newspaper?

W：Just put it in the bag with the rest of the trash.

M：You should separate your garbage.

W：It's too much trouble.

M：But it's good for the environment and it will save you money, too.

Question：What does the man want the woman to do?

A. Stop wasting money.

B. Stop buying the newspaper.

C. Recycle her trash.

* put〔pʊt〕*v.* 放　　old〔old〕*adj.* 老舊的

newspaper〔'njuz,pepə〕*n.* 報紙

just〔dʒʌst〕*adv.* 就…（委婉的祈使語氣）

bag〔bæg〕*n.* 袋子　　rest〔rɛst〕*n.* 剩餘

trash〔træʃ〕*n.* 垃圾

separate〔'sɛpə,ret〕*v.* 把…分開

garbage〔'garbɪdʒ〕*n.* 垃圾

trouble〔'trʌbl̩〕*n.* 麻煩

environment〔ɪn'vaɪrənmənt〕*n.* 環境

save〔sev〕*v.* 節省　　stop〔stɑp〕*v.* 停止

waste〔west〕*v.* 浪費　　recycle〔ri'saɪkl̩〕*v.* 回收

28. (**B**) W：I'm going for a walk.

M：You should wear something with long sleeves.

W：Why? It's not that cold.

M：But there are lots of mosquitoes.

Question：Why does the man suggest the woman put on more clothes?

A. It is going to rain.

B. She might get bitten.

C. She might get cold.

* **go for a walk** 去散步　　long〔lɔŋ〕adj. 長的

　sleeve〔sliv〕n. 袖子　　that〔ðæt〕adv. 那麼地

　lots of 很多　　mosquito〔mə'skito〕n. 蚊子

　suggest〔səg'dʒɛst〕v. 建議

　put on 穿上　　more〔mor〕adj. 更多的

　might〔maɪt〕aux. 可能

　bite〔baɪt〕v. 咬（三態變化爲：bite-bit-bitten）

　get bitten 被咬　　**get cold** 感冒

29.(**C**)　W：How do you pronounce this word?

　　M：Sorry, I don't know. Did you look in the dictionary?

　　W：Yes, but it's not much help.

　　Question：What does the woman want to know?

　　A. How to find the word in the dictionary.

　　B. How to write the word.

　　C. How to say the word.

* pronounce〔prə'naʊns〕v. 發…的音

　dictionary〔'dɪkʃən͵ɛrɪ〕n. 字典

　help〔hɛlp〕n. 幫助

　find〔faɪnd〕v. 找到

30. (**B**) W: When are you going to Japan?

　　　 M: I leave on the thirtieth.

　　　 W: And how long will you stay there?

　　　 M: I'll return on the second.

　　　 Question: How long will the man stay in Japan?

　　　 A. Seven days.

　　　 B. Only a few days.

　　　 C. More than two weeks.

　　　 * Japan〔dʒə'pæn〕 *n.* 日本　　 leave〔liv〕 *v.* 離開

　　　 thirtieth〔'θɜtɪɪθ〕 *n.* (每月的)三十日

　　　 How long~? ～多久？　　 stay〔ste〕 *v.* 停留

　　　 return〔rɪ'tɜn〕 *v.* 返回

　　　 second〔'sɛkənd〕 *n.* (每月的)二日

　　　 a few 一些；幾個

　　　 more than 超過(= *over*)

二、閱讀能力測驗

第一部份：詞彙和結構

1. (**A**) <u>What kind of</u> drink do you like the most?
　　　 你最喜歡<u>什麼種類的</u>飲料？

　　　 a kind of 作「一種…」解，故 (B) what a kind of 和 (D)
　　　 what kind of a 文法錯誤。題目是問「什麼種類的飲
　　　 料」，即從「眾多」飲料中選出最喜歡的，故飲料種類
　　　 應不只一種，故 (C) what kind 用法不合。

　　　 * drink〔drɪŋk〕 *n.* 飲料

2. (**B**)　I have so <u>little</u> time to prepare for the final exam.

我只有這麼<u>少的</u>時間準備期末考。

(A) few（很少）以及 (C) a few（一些）後只可接「可數名詞」，故在此用法不合。(B) little（很少的）以及 (D) a little（一些的）後只可接「不可數名詞」，但因空格前有一副詞 so（如此地），故應選 (B)，解作「如此少的」，較合理。

* prepare〔prɪ'pɛr〕v. 準備
  final〔'faɪnl̩〕adj. 最後的　　*final exam*　期末考

3. (**D**)　Joan is the most skillful hairdresser <u>that</u> I have ever seen.　瓊是我見過的美髮師中，技巧最好的。

若先行詞之前有最高級形容詞時，關係代名詞只能用 that，故選 (D)。

* skillful〔'skɪlfəl〕adj. 技術精湛的
  hairdresser〔'hɛr,drɛsɚ〕n. 美髮師
  ever〔'ɛvɚ〕adv. 曾經

4. (**B**)　Call an <u>ambulance</u>, please! Someone is hurt.

請叫<u>救護車</u>！有人受傷了。

(A) alphabet〔'ælfə,bɛt〕n. 字母（表）
(B) *ambulance*〔'æmbjələns〕n. 救護車
(C) accident〔'æksədənt〕n. 意外
(D) actress〔'æktrɪs〕n. 女演員

* call〔kɔl〕v. 叫　　hurt〔hɝt〕adj. 受傷的

5. (**D**) Give up smoking, or it will <u>affect</u> your health.

戒煙吧，否則會<u>影響</u>你的健康。

    (A) offer〔'ɔfɚ〕*v.* 提供

    (B) improve〔ɪm'pruv〕*v.* 改進

    (C) increase〔ɪn'kris〕*v.* 增加

    (D) ***affect***〔ə'fɛkt〕*v.* 影響

    * ***give up*** 放棄   smoking〔'smokɪŋ〕*n.* 抽煙

    or〔ɔr〕*conj.* 否則   health〔hɛlθ〕*n.* 健康

6. (**D**) I need shrimp. Could you go to the <u>supermarket</u> and buy some for me?

我需要蝦子。你可以去<u>超級市場</u>幫我買一些嗎？

    (A) convenience store 便利商店

    (B) stationery store 文具店

    (C) post office 郵局

    (D) ***supermarket***〔'supɚ‚markɪt〕*n.* 超級市場

    * shrimp〔ʃrɪmp〕*n.* 蝦子

    stationery〔'steʃən‚ɛrɪ〕*n.* 文具

7. (**A**) Guava is a bit hard. <u>Why not</u> eat something softer?

芭樂有點硬。<u>為什麼不</u>吃軟一點的東西？

    Why not~?是 Why don't + 主詞~?的簡略說法，為一表提議的口語用法。因空格後沒有主詞，故應選 (A)。

    * guava〔'gwɑvə〕*n.* 芭樂   ***a bit*** 有一點

    hard〔hɑrd〕*adj.* 硬的

    softer〔'sɔftɚ〕*adj.* 較軟的（soft 的比較級）

8. (**C**) We will go mountain climbing if it <u>is</u> a clear day this
Sunday. 如果這個星期天<u>是</u>晴天的話，我們將會去爬山。

表「條件」的副詞子句，應以現在式代替未來式，故選 (C)。

* ***mountain climbing*** 登山　　clear〔klɪr〕*adj.* 晴朗的

9. (**B**) <u>This is</u> Jeff. Is Bruce there? I want to talk to him.
<u>我是</u>傑夫。布魯斯在嗎？我想跟他說話。

在電話中，表明自己的身份時，通常用 This is…，故
選 (B)。

10. (**A**) Let's go for a walk, <u>shall</u> we?
我們去散步，<u>好嗎</u>？

以 Let's 開頭的句子，附加問句中的助動詞，一律用
shall，故選 (A)。

* ***go for a walk*** 去散步

11. (**C**) Chris : Do you like my new necktie?
Jesse : Yes, very much. I'll buy <u>one</u> for my father.
克里斯：你喜歡我新買的領帶嗎？
傑　西：是的，非常喜歡。我要買<u>一條</u>給我爸。

it 和 one 都可用以代替前面已提過的名詞，兩者的差別在
於：it 所指的事物，和前面所提到的是同一個；而 one 所
代表的名詞，和前面所提到的名詞是同一類，並非指同一
個。傑西要買一條和克里斯一模一樣的領帶，而非向克里
斯買他所擁有的那條領帶，故應選 (C) ***one***。(B) a 是形容
詞，在此不合。若選 (D) the other (necktie)「另外一條
（領帶）」，則不合句意。　　* necktie〔'nɛkˌtaɪ〕*n.* 領帶

12. (**A**)　George is the thinnest of us all.
　　　　　喬治是<u>我們全部</u>之中最瘦的。

　　　　　　all 與代名詞連用時，當同位格用，須放在代名詞後，且
　　　　　　介系詞 of 後應接受詞，故選 (A)。

　　　　　　* thinnest〔'θɪnɪst〕*adj.* 最瘦的（thin 的最高級）

13. (**B**)　Danny was lucky <u>enough</u> to win the lottery.
　　　　　丹尼真是幸運得<u>足以</u>中樂透。

　　　　　　「be 動詞 + 形容詞 + enough + to V.」表「～得足以…」，
　　　　　　故選 (B)。而 (A) much 當副詞時，通常放在動詞後修飾，
　　　　　　而非形容詞後，(C) very 通常只放在其所修飾的名詞之前，
　　　　　　(D) 有 Danny was lucky a lot. 的寫法，但其後不可再加不
　　　　　　定詞，故不合。

　　　　　　* lucky〔'lʌkɪ〕*adj.* 幸運的
　　　　　　　win〔wɪn〕*v.* 贏（三態變化為：win-won-won）
　　　　　　　lottery〔'lɑtərɪ〕*n.* 樂透彩

14. (**C**)　Peter is a dishonest person. I don't trust him <u>at all</u>.
　　　　　彼得是個不誠實的人，我<u>一點也</u>不相信他。

　　　　　　(A) after all　畢竟
　　　　　　(B) in all　總計
　　　　　　(C) *at all*　一點也（不）
　　　　　　(D) for all　儘管

　　　　　　* dishonest〔dɪs'ɑnɪst〕*adj.* 不誠實的
　　　　　　　trust〔trʌst〕*v.* 信任

15. (**D**) Will you <u>do</u> me a favor? I can't start my car.

　　　你可以<u>幫</u>我個忙嗎？我的車子發不動。

　　　「幫某人的忙」可用 *do sb. a favor*，故選 (D)。

　　　* start〔stɑrt〕*v.* 發動

第二部份：段落填空

<u>Questions 16-19</u>

Sam: This menu has a lot of good <u>dishes</u>. In fact, everything
　　　　　　　　　　　　　　　　　　　 16

　　　<u>looks</u> delicious. I'm going to have the roast beef.
　　　 17

Tom: I've <u>gained</u> a few pounds lately. I'm going to have fish
　　　　　　 18

　　　and salad.

Sam: Tom, you're so thin. You don't have to <u>diet</u>. Look at
　　　　　　　　　　　　　　　　　　　　　　 19

　　　me! I'm the one who should eat fish and salad.

山姆：這菜單上有好多很好的菜餚。事實上，每一樣看起來都很好吃。
　　　我要吃烤牛肉。

湯姆：我最近胖了幾磅。我要吃魚和沙拉。

山姆：湯姆，你很瘦。你不需要節食。看看我！我才是那個應該吃魚
　　　和沙拉的人。

　　　menu〔'mɛnju〕*n.* 菜單　　***in fact*** 事實上
　　　delicious〔dɪ'lɪʃəs〕*adj.* 美味的
　　　have〔hæv〕*v.* 吃；喝　　roast〔rost〕*adj.* 烤過的
　　　beef〔bif〕*n.* 牛肉　　***a few*** 幾個；一些
　　　pound〔paʊnd〕*n.* 磅　　lately〔'letlɪ〕*adv.* 最近
　　　have〔hæv〕*v.* 吃　　fish〔fɪʃ〕*n.* 魚
　　　salad〔'sæləd〕*n.* 沙拉　　so〔so〕*adv.* 如此地
　　　thin〔θɪn〕*adj.* 瘦的　　***look at*** 看

16. (**C**)　(A) snack〔snæk〕 *n.* 點心　　(B) cook〔kʊk〕 *n.* 廚師

　　　　　(C) ***dish***〔dɪʃ〕 *n.* 菜餚　　(D) price〔praɪs〕 *n.* 價格

17. (**D**)　(A) cook〔kʊk〕 *v.* 烹調　　(B) check〔tʃɛk〕 *v.* 檢查

　　　　　(C) choose〔tʃuz〕 *v.* 選擇　　(D) ***look***〔lʊk〕 *v.* 看起來

18. (**B**)　(A) win〔wɪn〕 *v.* 贏（三態變化為：win-won-won）

　　　　　(B) ***gain***〔gen〕 *v.* 增加

　　　　　(C) lift〔lɪft〕 *v.* 舉起

　　　　　(D) raise〔rez〕 *v.* 提高；舉起

19. (**B**)　(A) eat〔it〕 *v.* 吃　　　　(B) ***diet***〔'daɪət〕 *v.* 進行節食

　　　　　(C) cook〔kʊk〕 *v.* 烹調　　(D) wash dishes　洗碗盤

Questions 20-25

　　Thomas Edison was a famous American inventor.　When he was a child, he was always trying out new <u>ideas</u>.　Young
　　　　　　　　　　　　　　　　　　　　　　　　20
Edison was <u>in school</u> for only three months.　During those three
　　　　　　　21
months he asked his teacher a lot of questions.　Most of the questions were not about his lessons.　His teacher thought he wasn't <u>clever</u> and told his mother to take him out of school.
　　　　　22
Edison's mother had to teach him <u>herself</u>.　Edison learnt very
　　　　　　　　　　　　　　　　23
quickly.　He read a lot.　Later he became very interested in <u>science</u> and invented many <u>useful</u> things.
　24　　　　　　　　　　　　　　25

　　湯瑪斯愛迪生是一個有名的美國發明家。當他還是個小孩子的時候，他總是會試驗新的想法。年輕的愛迪生只上學三個月。在那三個月期間，他問他的老師很多問題，大部分的問題都和所上的課無關。他的老師認為他不聰明，並告訴他的媽媽，把他帶離學校。愛迪生的媽媽必須自己教他。愛迪生學得很快，他讀很多書。後來，他變得對科學非常有興趣，並發明了很多有用的東西。

famous〔'feməs〕*adj.* 有名的
American〔ə'mɛrɪkən〕*adj.* 美國的
inventor〔ɪn'vɛntɚ〕*n.* 發明家　　***try out*** 試驗
during〔'djʊrɪŋ〕*prep.* 在…期間
most of… 大部分的…　　lesson〔'lɛsṇ〕*n.* 課程
think〔θɪŋk〕*v.* 認為　　later〔'letɚ〕*adv.* 後來
become〔bɪ'kʌm〕*v.* 變得
interested〔'ɪntrɪstɪd〕*adj.* 感興趣的
invent〔ɪn'vɛnt〕*v.* 發明

20. (**B**) (A) answer〔'ænsɚ〕*n.* 答案
　　　　(B) ***idea***〔aɪ'diə〕*n.* 想法
　　　　(C) question〔'kwɛstʃən〕*n.* 問題
　　　　(D) way〔we〕*n.* 方法

21. (**C**) (A) at home　在家　　　　(B) on the farm　在農場上
　　　　(C) ***in school***　上學　　　(D) by the river　在河邊

22. (**D**) (A) kind〔kaɪnd〕*adj.* 仁慈的
　　　　(B) ***clever***〔'klɛvɚ〕*adj.* 聰明的
　　　　(C) bad〔bæd〕*adj.* 不好的
　　　　(D) forgetful〔fɚ'gɛtfəl〕*adj.* 健忘的

23. (**D**) 反身代名詞可放在主詞後，或句尾，用以強調主詞本身，這句話的主詞是 Edison's mother，第三人稱女性，故選 (D) ***herself***。

(A) a lesson 一個教訓　　(B) lonely 〔ˋlonlɪ〕 *adj.* 寂寞的

24. (**A**) (A) ***science*** 〔ˋsaɪəns〕 *n.* 科學
(B) art 〔ɑrt〕 *n.* 藝術
(C) history 〔ˋhɪstrɪ〕 *n.* 歷史
(D) music 〔ˋmjuzɪk〕 *n.* 音樂

25. (**D**) (A) terrible 〔ˋtɛrəbḷ〕 *adj.* 可怕的
(B) common 〔ˋkɑmən〕 *adj.* 一般的；常見的
(C) chemical 〔ˋkɛmɪkḷ〕 *adj.* 化學的
(D) ***useful*** 〔ˋjusfəl〕 *adj.* 有用的

第三部份：閱讀理解

Question 26

```
請勿踐踏草坪
```

keep off 不進入　　grass 〔græs〕 *n.* 草；草坪

26. (**D**) 此告示牌是什麼意思？

(A) 請多種一些草。　　　(B) 把草存放在安全的地方。
(C) 不要離開草坪。　　　(D) 不要走上草坪。

* sign 〔saɪn〕 *n.* 告示牌　　mean 〔min〕 *v.* 意思是
plant 〔plænt〕 *v.* 種植　　keep 〔kip〕 *v.* 把⋯存放
safe 〔sef〕 *adj.* 安全的　　leave 〔liv〕 *v.* 離開

Questions 27-29

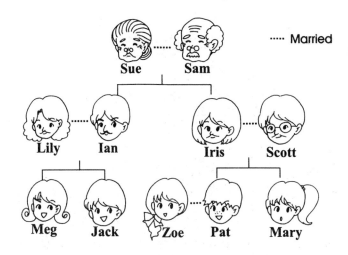

27. (**C**) 誰是瑪莉的堂（表）兄弟姊妹？

　　(A) 莉莉。　　　　　　　(B) 伊安。
　　(C) 傑克。　　　　　　　(D) 柔伊。

　　* cousin〔'kʌzn̩〕n. 堂（表）兄弟姊妹

28. (**C**) 誰是史考特的姪女？

　　(A) 莉莉。　　　　　　　(B) 傑克。
　　(C) 梅格。　　　　　　　(D) 伊安。

　　* niece〔nis〕n. 姪女

29. (**C**) 誰是瑪莉的嫂嫂或弟妹？

　　(A) 莉莉。　　　　　　　(B) 梅格。
　　(C) 柔伊。　　　　　　　(D) 沒有人。

　　* sister-in-law〔'sɪstərɪnˌlɔ〕n. 姻親的姊妹；嫂嫂；弟妹
　　　none〔nʌn〕pron. 沒有人

Questions 30-32

工作申請表

姓名：陳大衛
地址：新竹市大學路 123 號
電話：(03) 222-3456

高 中	成功高中
重要課程	電腦三年；數學四年；化學兩年
語 言	日文三年(讀、寫、說)；法文兩年 (讀、寫)
經 驗	送報紙；在史密斯餐廳當點餐人員
興 趣	我喜歡旅行和打籃球。放學後，我常和我的朋友打籃球，而且我通常會在假期時去旅行。我喜歡和人們一起工作，並幫助他們。

---

job〔dʒɑb〕n. 工作　application〔͵æplə'keʃən〕n. 申請；應徵
form〔fɔrm〕n. 表格　address〔ə'drɛs, 'ædrɛs〕n. 地址
phone number 電話號碼　key〔ki〕adj. 重要的；主要的
course〔kors〕n. 課程　computer〔kəm'pjutɚ〕n. 電腦
math〔mæθ〕n. 數學 (= *mathematics*)
chemistry〔'kɛmɪstrɪ〕n. 化學　Japanese〔͵dʒæpə'niz〕n. 日文
reading〔'ridɪŋ〕n. 閱讀　writing〔'raɪtɪŋ〕n. 書寫
speaking〔'spikɪŋ〕n. 說　French〔frɛntʃ〕n. 法文
experience〔ɪk'spɪrɪəns〕n. 經驗　deliver〔dɪ'lɪvɚ〕v. 遞送

newspaper (ˈnjuzˌpepɚ) n. 報紙　　order (ˈɔrdɚ) n. 點 (的菜)
take food order 記下 (客人) 點的菜
Smith's 史密斯餐廳 (= *Smith's Restaurant*)
interest (ˈɪntrɪst) n. 興趣　　traveling (ˈtrævlɪŋ) n. 旅行
holiday (ˈhɑləˌde) n. 假日　　enjoy (ɪnˈdʒɔɪ) v. 喜歡

30. (**C**)　在表格裡我們找不到陳大衛的＿＿＿＿＿＿。

　　　(A) interest (ˈɪntrɪst) n. 興趣
　　　(B) address (əˈdrɛs , ˈædrɛs) n. 地址
　　　(C) ***age*** (edʒ) n. 年齡
　　　(D) experience (ɪkˈspɪrɪəns) n. 經驗

31. (**A**)　他曾經在哪裡工作過？

　　　(A) 在餐廳。　　　　　　(B) 在警察局。
　　　(C) 在郵局。　　　　　　(D) 在電腦公司。

　　　* ever (ˈɛvɚ) adv. 曾經
　　　　restaurant (ˈrɛstərənt) n. 餐廳
　　　　police station 警察局　***post office*** 郵局
　　　　company (ˈkʌmpənɪ) n. 公司

32. (**D**)　大衛最喜歡的運動是什麼？

　　　(A) 電腦。　　　　　　　(B) 旅行。
　　　(C) 數學。　　　　　　　(D) 籃球。

　　　* favorite (ˈfevərɪt) adj. 最喜愛的
　　　　exercise (ˈɛksɚˌsaɪz) n. 運動

Questions 33-35

First invented in the 1940s, TV became very popular in the 1950s. By 1960, almost every U.S. living room had a TV. For over fifty years now, television has influenced the way we live.

電視最早發明於四〇年代，到了五〇年代變得非常受歡迎。到了六〇年代，幾乎每一個美國家庭的客廳，都有一台電視。電視影響了我們的生活方式，到現在已經超過五十年了。

> invent〔ɪn'vɛnt〕v. 發明
> *in the 1940s* 在一九四〇年代（指 1940～1949 年）
> become〔bɪ'kʌm〕v. 變得　　popular〔'pɑpjələ〕adj. 受歡迎的
> by〔baɪ〕prep. 到了　　almost〔'ɔl,most〕adv. 幾乎
> *U.S.* 美國（= *United States*）
> over〔'ovə〕prep. 超過（= *more than*）
> now〔naʊ〕adv. 現在（已經）　　influence〔'ɪnfluəns〕v. 影響
> way〔we〕n. 方式　　live〔lɪv〕v. 生活

Children are most affected by television. This worries many parents and teachers because most TV programs have no educational value. Cartoons and violent programs are entertaining, but have no benefits. The biggest worry of parents and teachers is that TV causes lower math and reading scores. Because of so much time spent watching TV, children are spending less time reading and thinking independently.

小孩子受電視的影響最大，這讓許多父母和老師擔心，因為大部分的電視節目都沒有教育的價值。卡通節目和暴力節目是有趣，但是並沒有益處。父母和老師最擔心的是，電視造成數學和閱讀的成績降低。因為孩子花太多的時間看電視，花較少的時間閱讀和獨立思考。

affect〔əˋfɛkt〕v. 影響　　worry〔ˋwɝɪ〕v. 使擔心　n. 擔心

parents〔ˋpɛrənts〕n. pl. 父母　　most〔most〕adj. 大部分的

program〔ˋprogræm〕n. 節目

educational〔͵ɛdʒəˋkeʃənḷ〕adj. 教育的

value〔ˋvæljʊ〕n. 價值　　cartoon〔kɑrˋtun〕n. 卡通

violent〔ˋvaɪələnt〕adj. 暴力的

entertaining〔͵ɛntəˋtenɪŋ〕adj. 有趣的；令人愉快的

benefit〔ˋbɛnəfɪt〕n. 益處　　biggest〔ˋbɪgɪst〕adj. 最大的

cause〔kɔz〕v. 造成　　lower〔ˋloɚ〕adj. 較低的

score〔skor〕n. 分數　　*because of* 因為

spend〔spɛnd〕v. 花（時間）　　less〔lɛs〕adj. 較少的

independently〔͵ɪndɪˋpɛndəntlɪ〕adv. 獨立地

Kids in America watch more than two hours of TV a day on weekdays and over five hours a day on weekends. Experts say that if we all want to do better and be better, we must limit our TV watching.

美國的孩子在平日，一天看兩個小時以上的電視，在週末，一天看超過五個小時的電視。專家說，如果我們想要做得更好，或變得更好，我們就必須限制我們看電視的時間。

kid〔kɪd〕n. 小孩　　America〔əˋmɛrɪkə〕n. 美國

more than 超過　　weekday〔ˋwik͵de〕n. 平日

weekend〔ˋwikˋɛnd〕n. 週末　　expert〔ˋɛkspɝt〕n. 專家

better〔ˋbɛtɚ〕adv. 比較好　adj. 比較好的

limit〔ˋlɪmɪt〕v. 限制

33. (**C**) 為什麼父母和老師擔心電視？

    (A) 因為小孩會變得很危險。

    (B) 因為犯罪事件增加。

    (C) <u>因為考試成績越來越低。</u>

    (D) 因為卡通太無聊了。

    * dangerous〔'dendʒərəs〕adj. 危險的
       crime〔kraɪm〕n. 犯罪
       rise〔raɪz〕v. 上升
       grade〔gred〕n. 成績
       get〔gɛt〕v. 變得
       boring〔'borɪŋ〕adj. 無聊的

34. (**C**) 大部分的美國人什麼時候有電視？

    (A) 超過一百年以前。

    (B) 超過七十年以前。

    (C) <u>在五〇年代。</u>

    (D) 在四〇年代。

    * century〔'sɛntʃərɪ〕n. 世紀

35. (**D**) 美國的小孩一個星期大約看幾個小時的電視？

    (A) 超過四十小時。

    (B) 三十小時左右。

    (C) 十四小時。

    (D) <u>約二十小時。</u>

    * around〔ə'raʊnd〕adv. …左右

全民英語能力分級檢定測驗
初級測驗④

一、聽力測驗

　　本測驗分三部份，全為三選一之選擇題，每部份各 10 題，共 30 題，作答時間約 20 分鐘。

第一部份：看圖辨義

　　　　　本部份共10題，試題冊上每題有一個圖片，請聽錄音機播出一個相關的問題，與 A、B、C 三個英語敘述後，選一個與所看到圖片最相符的答案，並在答案紙上相對的圓圈內塗黑作答。每題播出一遍，問題及選項均不印在試題冊上。

例：（看）

（聽）

Look at the picture.　How much is the hamburger?

　　A.　It's eighty dollars.

　　B.　It's fifty-five dollars.

　　C.　It's eighteen dollars.

正確答案為 A

A. <u>Question 1</u>

B. <u>Questions 2-3</u>

C. **Question 4**

D. **Question 5**

E. **Question 6**

請 翻 頁 ⇒

F. **Question 7**

G. **Question 8**

H. Question 9

I. Question 10

請 翻 頁 ⟹

第二部份：問答

本部份共 10 題，每題錄音機會播出一個問句或直述句，每題播出一次，聽後請從試題冊上 A、B、C 三個選項中，選出一個最適合的回答或回應，並在答案紙上塗黑作答。

例：

（聽）　Good morning, Kevin. How are you?

（看）　A.　I'm fine, thank you.
　　　　B.　I'm in the living room.
　　　　C.　My name is Kevin.

正確答案為 A

11. A. We were rather
　　　poor.
　　B. I grew up in Hong
　　　Kong.
　　C. I had a very happy
　　　childhood.

12. A. I had fun, too.
　　B. Drive carefully.
　　C. Here. Take my
　　　sunglasses.

13. A. No, she came home
　　　last week.
　　B. Yes, she's older than me.
　　C. No, she is studying
　　　abroad now.

14. A. Yes, I enjoy the view.
　　B. Yes, I'm so glad that I
　　　bought one.
　　C. Yes, it's more
　　　convenient than driving.

15. A. Yes, I'm having a
　　　party.
　　B. No, I had to cancel
　　　it.
　　C. Yes, but I can't go.

16. A. Which page?
　　B. Sorry. I'll read
　　　silently.
　　C. It's about the game
　　　last night.

17. A. The winners will be
　　　announced during
　　　the show.
　　B. They are held in
　　　California.
　　C. We can see the show
　　　on Sunday.

18. A. Yes, he's my cousin.
　　B. No, he's not my
　　　neighbor.
　　C. Yes, my nickname is
　　　Johnny.

19. A. Here's a match.
　　B. Don't worry. He knows
　　　how to get there.
　　C. You should have tied
　　　him up.

20. A. Yes, I often watch TV
　　　news.
　　B. Not often. I'm more
　　　interested in my
　　　hometown.
　　C. No, I've never been
　　　abroad.

請 翻 頁

第三部份： 簡短對話

本部份共 10 題，每題錄音機會播出一段對話及一個相關的問題，每題播出兩次，聽後請從試題冊上 A、B、C 三個選項中，選出一個最適合的回答，並在答案紙上塗黑作答。

例：

（聽） (Woman) Good afternoon, …Mr. Davis?

(Man) Yes. I have an appointment with Dr. Sanders at two o'clock. My son Tommy has a fever.

(Woman) Oh, that's too bad. Well, please have a seat, Mr. Davis. Dr. Sanders will be right with you.

Question: Where did this conversation take place?

（看） A. In a post office.

B. In a restaurant.

C. In a doctor's office.

正確答案爲 C

21. A. At 11:00 a.m.
    B. At 11:30 p.m.
    C. In half an hour.

22. A. He wishes he had a new iPod.
    B. He is happy for the woman.
    C. He wants to borrow the woman's iPod.

23. A. When the Ming dynasty ended.
    B. What elements water is composed of.
    C. The names of the countries of Africa.

24. A. His brother is not sure whether or not he will get married.
    B. His brother's girlfriend is not eager to get married.
    C. His brother will get married after he graduates.

25. A. She finished her studies.
    B. She couldn't find a suitable place to live.
    C. She missed her friends and family.

請 翻 頁 ▯⟹

26. A. Geography.
    B. Science.
    C. University.

27. A. Pay attention to her
       dog.
    B. Pay no attention to
       the barking dog.
    C. Find out why the
       dog is barking.

28. A. Get her a drink.
    B. Give her some coins.
    C. Change his order.

29. A. The man bought the
       plant a few months
       ago.
    B. The man planted the
       plant himself.
    C. The woman does not
       know how many
       seeds to plant.

30. A. Worried.
    B. Cold.
    C. Calm.

二、閱讀能力測驗

本測驗分三部份，全為四選一之選擇題，共 35 題，作答時間 35 分鐘。

第一部份： 詞彙和結構

本部份共15題，每題含一個空格。請就試題冊上 A、B、C、D 四個選項中選出最適合題意的字或詞，標示在答案紙上。

1. Nara forgot _____ her dinner, so she ate at 11 p.m.
   A. eating
   B. ate
   C. to eat
   D. have eaten

2. I'll _____ a light on for you if you come home late.
   A. leave
   B. take
   C. do
   D. make

3. It was raining, so my mother didn't allow me to swim _____ the river.
   A. on
   B. in
   C. by
   D. at

請 翻 頁 ▷

4. The little girl who is walking a dog is my _____.
   A. niece
   B. nephew
   C. aunt
   D. female

5. My teacher _____ many spelling mistakes in my English composition.
   A. indicated
   B. inspired
   C. interrupted
   D. invented

6 I am just an _____ person. I just want a regular life.
   A. evil
   B. ordinary
   C. excellent
   D. intelligent

7. Jason : My secretary didn't _____ yesterday's meeting.
   Jane : You mean she was absent from the meeting.
   A. enter
   B. prepare
   C. report
   D. attend

8. J.K. Rowling is one of the _____ writers in the world.

    A. famousest

    B. more famouser

    C. most famous

    D. much famous

9. Mary is not smart _____ diligent.

    A. too

    B. than

    C. as

    D. but

10. _____ do I stay at home during holidays.

    A. Usually

    B. Seldom

    C. How

    D. Almost

11. Jason : Didn't you take the garbage out yet?

    Jane : _____. The garbage truck hasn't come yet.

    A. Yes, I do

    B. Yes, I didn't

    C. No, I did

    D. No, I didn't

請 翻 頁 ▯▭⟹

12. I am used to _____ my teeth before going to bed.

A. brush

B. brushing

C. have brushed

D. brushed

13. Dinah has lived in Ilan _____ 1981.

A. before

B. in

C. since

D. for

14. The baby was made _____ by the big noise.

A. cry

B. cried

C. to cry

D. crying

15. It's _____ a nice day that many people are going on a picnic.

A. so

B. such

C. very

D. as

第二部份： 段落填空

　　本部份共 10 題，包括二個段落，每個段落各含 5 個空格。請就試題冊上 A、B、C、D 四個選項中選出最適合題意的字或詞，標示在答案紙上。

Questions 16-20

　　Last Friday I got really wet from head to ___(16)___. After ___(17)___ work, I left ___(18)___ home on my old bicycle. I was going fast because it was ___(19)___ to rain. After five minutes, my bike broke down ___(20)___ a strange noise. Just then, it started to rain. I walked my bike home quickly in the rain. I didn't complain because I didn't get hurt. ___(21)___, it felt kind of refreshing to feel the water washing down on me.

16. A. ankle
　　 B. wrist
　　 C. elbow
　　 D. toe

17. A. had finished
　　 B. finished
　　 C. finishing
　　 D. to finish

18. A. to
　　 B. for
　　 C. of
　　 D. in

19. A. started
　　 B. about
　　 C. stopped
　　 D. almost

請翻頁

20. A. of
    B. in
    C. with
    D. by

21. A. Actually
    B. Usually
    C. Finally
    D. Probably

Questions 22-25

The second ___(22)___ started today. It was very hard ___(23)___ me to get up at six-thirty this morning. But it was nice to see my classmates again after one month. The first class was math. I'm not good ___(24)___ math, so I felt the period was very long. After school, my tennis club had a meeting. After the meeting, we spent an hour ___(25)___ tennis.

22. A. class
    B. exam
    C. term
    D. season

24. A. for
    B. at
    C. on
    D. of

23. A. for
    B. to
    C. by
    D. of

25. A. to play
    B. play
    C. playing
    D. played

第三部份： 閱讀理解

本部份共 10 題，包括數段短文，每段短文後有 1～3 個相關問題，請就試題冊上 A、B、C、D 四個選項中選出最適合者，標示在答案紙上。

Question 26

Wanted

Full-Time

5 Days a Week

Experienced Baker

* * *

Stewart's Bakery

26. What kind of person does Stewart's Bakery need?

A. A full-time person to sell bread.

B. An employee who can manage a bakery.

C. An experienced cook.

D. A person who has worked many years baking things.

請 翻 頁 ▯▯⟹

Questions 27-29

The following chart（圖表）shows the results of a survey（調查）of parents from five countries who were asked why children are important to them. They were asked to choose three main reasons from seven. For example, the three most important reasons for Japanese parents are Item 4 —strengthening（加強）family ties (51%), Item 5 —developing oneself through raising one's children (60%), and Item 7 —raising responsible citizens (45%).

Items	Japan	Korea	U.S.A.	Britain	France
① To see oneself continuing on in future generations	35%	31%	32%	17%	59%
② To keep the family line	24%	68%	28%	17%	26%
③ To receive care in old age	10%	38%	8%	7%	8%
④ To strengthen family ties	51%	25%	50%	55%	66%
⑤ To develop oneself through raising one's children	60%	19%	54%	69%	35%
⑥ To enjoy raising children	20%	19%	50%	71%	39%
⑦ To raise responsible citizens	45%	40%	46%	28%	15%

27. Among all the countries, only _____ parents think that keeping the family line is the most important reason for raising children.

   A. American

   B. French

   C. Japanese

   D. Korean

28. Which item do the most countries think is one of their main reasons?

   A. Item 1.

   B. Item 4.

   C. Item 5.

   D. Item 6.

29. Which two countries have the same main reasons for raising children?

   A. Japan and Korea.

   B. America and Britain.

   C. Britain and France.

   D. Japan and America.

請 翻 頁 ▌⟹

Questions 30-32

April Apple Middle School				
Monday	**Tuesday**	**Wednesday**	**Thursday**	**Friday**
1/ School meeting	2/ Basketball Group meeting	3/ Art Show	4/ ⟶	5/ Picnic
8/ Computer Group Meeting	9/ Field Trip	10/ Singing Group Meeting	11/ English Group Meeting	12/ Baseball Group meeting
15/ School Meeting	16/ Half Day: Leave at Noon	17/ Film: Face Off	18/ Science Group Meeting	19/ Talent Show
22/ Exams	23/ ⟶	24/	25/	26/
29/ Graduation Meeting				

30. The students have a school meeting _____ in April.

    A. six times   B. three times

    C. twice   D. once

31. From the above chart（圖表）we can see that there are two
_____ groups in this school.
A. sports   B. art
C. science   D. language

32. How long does the art show last?
A. One day.   B. Two days.
C. Three days.   D. Four days.

Questions 33-35

Mozart was born in 1756. Everyone knows he was one
of the world's most famous music composers. Mozart had an
amazing early life. He was writing excellent music by the age
of five. At the age of six, he was playing for kings and queens
all over Europe. His talent and genius made him very famous.

However, Mozart's adult life was a difficult one. He
never really found a steady（穩定的）job that could last for
more than a year. He was too impatient to teach and most jobs
creating music were only part-time. Therefore, Mozart was
always struggling to find work. He often spent too much
money so that he often had to borrow money.

請 翻 頁 ▯⟹

It's a pity that Mozart died from a high fever and brief illness at the young age of 35. It is even sadder because he died poor and almost all alone.

33. What is an amazing thing that Mozart did?
    A. He only lived 35 years.
    B. He memorized many names and numbers.
    C. He performed in many countries.
    D. He taught music to kings and queens.

34. All during his life, Mozart had trouble _____.
    A. with his family
    B. finding pupils to teach
    C. with his hearing
    D. making and saving money

35. What finally happened to Mozart?
    A. He caught a fever and became deaf.
    B. An illness caused his early death.
    C. He died of loneliness.
    D. He was killed in an accident.

初級英檢模擬試題④詳解

一、聽力測驗

第一部份

For question number 1, please look at picture A.

1. (**C**) Why is she angry?
    A. He's having fun.
    B. She is talking on the phone.
    C. The music is too loud.
    * angry〔'æŋgrɪ〕adj. 生氣的　　*have fun* 玩樂
      talk on the phone 講電話
      loud〔laʊd〕adj. 大聲的

For questions number 2 and 3, please look at picture B.

2. (**B**) Where is the bakery?
    A. On the traffic circle.
    B. It's on a corner.
    C. Next to the playground.
    * bakery〔'bekərɪ〕n. 麵包店
      traffic〔'træfɪk〕n. 交通
      circle〔'sɝkl̩〕n. 圓圈　　*traffic circle* 圓環
      corner〔'kɔrnɚ〕n. 轉角　　*next to⋯* 在⋯旁邊
      playground〔'ple͵graʊnd〕n. 遊樂場；操場

3. (**A**)　Please look at picture B again.　Which is NOT on the
traffic circle?

    A.　The Cultural Center.

    B.　Post office.

    C.　Stationery store.

    * cultural (ˈkʌltʃərəl) *adj.* 文化的

      center (ˈsɛntɚ) *n.* 中心　　***cultural center*** 文化中心

      post office 郵局　　stationery (ˈsteʃən‚ɛrɪ) *n.* 文具

      stationery store 文具店

For question number 4, please look at picture C.

4. (**C**)　What is on the table?

    A.　They can't decide.

    B.　Two girls.

    C.　A menu and drinks.

    * table (ˈtebl̩) *n.* 桌子　　decide (dɪˈsaɪd) *v.* 決定

      menu (ˈmɛnju) *n.* 菜單　　drink (drɪŋk) *n.* 飲料

For question number 5, please look at picture D.

5. (**A**)　What happened at the park?

    A.　People littered everywhere.

    B.　It's a windy day.

    C.　Newspapers and cans.

    * happen (ˈhæpən) *v.* 發生　　litter (ˈlɪtɚ) *v.* 亂丟垃圾

      everywhere (ˈɛvrɪ‚hwɛr) *adv.* 到處

      windy (ˈwɪndɪ) *adj.* 風大的

      newspaper (ˈnjuz‚pepɚ) *n.* 報紙　　can (kæn) *n.* 罐子

For question number 6, please look at picture E.

6. (**B**) How does the medicine taste?

    A. It's powdered medicine.

    B. It tastes bitter.

    C. A glass of water.

    * medicine (ˈmɛdəsn̩) *n.* 藥   taste (test) *v.* 嚐起來

    powdered (ˈpaʊdəd) *adj.* 粉狀的

    bitter (ˈbɪtə) *adj.* 苦的   ***a glass of*** ~　一杯~

For question number 7, please look at picture F.

7. (**B**) What is the man going to do?

    A. At a post office.

    B. He will send the package.

    C. She will receive it.

    * ***post office*** 郵局   send (sɛnd) *v.* 寄

    package (ˈpækɪdʒ) *n.* 包裹

    receive (rɪˈsiv) *v.* 接到；收到

For question number 8, please look at picture G.

8. (**A**) How many generations are in the picture?

    A. Two.

    B. Three.

    C. Five.

    * generation (ˌdʒɛnəˈreʃən) *n.* 世代

For question number 9, please look at picture H.

9. (**C**) What is the doctor doing?

    A. He is having his body examined.

    B. Checking with the nurse.

    C. Listening to the boy's heart.

    * examine〔ɪg'zæmɪn〕*v.* 診察（身體）

     have one's body examined 接受身體的診察

     check〔tʃɛk〕*v.* 核對；對照　　***check with*** ~　向~核對

     nurse〔nɝs〕*n.* 護士　　　heart〔hɑrt〕*n.* 心臟

For question number 10, please look at picture I.

10. (**B**) What happened in this picture?

    A. He is trying to help her.

    B. The girl fell down.

    C. She pushed the boy.

    * try〔traɪ〕*v.* 試著　　***fall down*** 跌倒

     push〔puʃ〕*v.* 推

第二部份

11. (**B**) Where did you spend your childhood?

    A. We were rather poor.

    B. I grew up in Hong Kong.

    C. I had a very happy childhood.

    * spend〔spɛnd〕*v.* 度過（時間）

     childhood〔'tʃaɪld,hud〕*n.* 童年

     rather〔'ræðɚ〕*adv.* 相當　　poor〔pur〕*adj.* 窮的

     grow up 長大　　***Hong Kong***〔'hɑŋ'kɑŋ〕*n.* 香港

12. (**B**) It's very foggy today.
    A. I had fun, too.　　B. Drive carefully.
    C. Here. Take my sunglasses.

   * foggy (ˈfɑgɪ) adj. 多霧的　　**have fun** 玩得開心
     drive (draɪv) v. 開車　　carefully (ˈkɛrfəlɪ) adv. 小心地
     here (hɪr) interj. 喂 (用於引起別人的注意)
     take (tek) v. 拿
     sunglasses (ˈsʌnˌglæsɪz) n. pl. 太陽眼鏡

13. (**A**) Is your sister still overseas?
    A. No, she came home last week.
    B. Yes, she's older than me.
    C. No, she is studying abroad now.

   * still (stɪl) adv. 仍然　　overseas (ˈovɚˈsiz) adv. 在國外
     last week 上個星期
     older (ˈoldɚ) adj. 較老的 (old 的比較級)
     abroad (əˈbrɔd) adv. 在國外

14. (**C**) Do you take the subway to work?
    A. Yes, I enjoy the view.
    B. Yes, I'm so glad that I bought one.
    C. Yes, it's more convenient than driving.

   * take (tek) v. 搭乘 (交通工具)
     subway (ˈsʌbˌwe) n. 地下鐵
     enjoy (ɪnˈdʒɔɪ) v. 喜歡；享受
     view (vju) n. 風景　　**so…that~** 如此…以致於~
     glad (glæd) adj. 高興的
     convenient (kəˈvinjənt) adj. 方便的

15. (**C**) Did you receive an invitation to the party?

    A. Yes, I'm having a party.

    B. No, I had to cancel it.

    C. Yes, but I can't go.

    * receive〔rɪˈsiv〕v. 接到；收到

      invitation〔ˌɪnvəˈteʃən〕n. 邀請函   have〔hæv〕v. 舉行

      have to 必須   cancel〔ˈkænsl̩〕v. 取消

16. (**B**) Please don't read aloud.

    A. Which page?

    B. Sorry. I'll read silently.

    C. It's about the game last night.

    * read〔rid〕v. 讀   aloud〔əˈlaʊd〕adv. 出聲地

      which〔hwɪtʃ〕adj. 哪一個   page〔pedʒ〕n. 頁

      silently〔ˈsaɪləntlɪ〕adv. 不出聲地

      game〔gem〕n. 比賽

17. (**C**) When will the Oscars be broadcast?

    A. The winners will be announced during the show.

    B. They are held in California.

    C. We can see the show on Sunday.

    * Oscar〔ˈɔskɚ〕n. 奧斯卡金像獎

      broadcast〔ˈbrɔdˌkæst〕v. 播出

      winner〔ˈwɪnɚ〕n. 優勝者；得獎者

      announce〔əˈnaʊns〕v. 公布；宣布

      during〔ˈdjʊrɪŋ〕prep. 在…期間

      show〔ʃo〕n. 節目   hold〔hold〕v. 舉行

      California〔ˌkæləˈfɔrnjə〕n. 加州

18. (**A**) Is Johnny a relative of yours?

A. Yes, he's my cousin.

B. No, he's not my neighbor.

C. Yes, my nickname is Johnny.

 * relative (ˈrɛlətɪv) *n.* 親戚
   yours (jʊrz) *pron.* you 的所有格代名詞
     (在此表「你的親戚」)
   cousin (ˈkʌzn̩) *n.* 表 (堂) 兄弟姊妹
   neighbor (ˈnebɚ) *n.* 鄰居
   nickname (ˈnɪkˌnem) *n.* 綽號

19. (**A**) Uh-oh. The candle has gone out.

A. Here's a match.

B. Don't worry. He knows how to get there.

C. You should have tied him up.

 * uh-oh (ˈʌˈo) *interj.* 唔哦 (遭遇問題時的感嘆語)
   candle (ˈkændl̩) *n.* 蠟燭
   go out 熄滅　　***Here is*** ~. 這裡有～。
   match (mætʃ) *n.* 火柴
   worry (ˈwɝɪ) *v.* 擔心
   get (gɛt) *v.* 抵達
   should have + ***p.p.*** 當初應該 (表過去該做而未做)
   tie (taɪ) *v.* 綁　　***tie up*** 綁起來

20. (**B**) Do you read the international news?

　　A. Yes, I often watch TV news.

　　B. Not often. I'm more interested in my hometown.

　　C. No, I've never been abroad.

　　* international 〔ˌɪntɚˈnæʃənḷ〕 *adj.* 國際的
　　news 〔njuz〕 *n.* 新聞　　often 〔ˈɔfən〕 *adv.* 經常
　　interested 〔ˈɪntrɪstɪd〕 *adj.* 感興趣
　　be interested in… 對…感興趣的
　　hometown 〔ˈhomˈtaʊn〕 *n.* 家鄉
　　abroad 〔əˈbrɔd〕 *adv.* 到國外
　　I've never been abroad. 我從沒出過國。

第三部份

21. (**B**) M：When should we leave for the train station?

　　W：Our train leaves at midnight.

　　M：Okay. Let's leave here half an hour before.

　　W：Good idea.

　　Question：When will they leave for the train station?

　　A. At 11:00 a.m.　　　　B. At 11:30 p.m.

　　C. In half an hour.

　　* ***leave for*** 動身前往　　***train station*** 火車站
　　leave 〔liv〕 *v.* 離開；出發
　　midnight 〔ˈmɪdˌnaɪt〕 *n.* 半夜；凌晨十二點
　　okay 〔ˈoˈke〕 *adv.* 好 (= *OK*)
　　half an hour before 早半個小時
　　idea 〔aɪˈdiə〕 *n.* 主意
　　a.m. 〔ˈeˈɛm〕 *adv.* 早上 (= *A.M.*)
　　p.m. 〔ˈpiˈɛm〕 *adv.* 下午 (= *P.M.*)
　　in half an hour 再過半小時

22. (**A**)　M：Is that your new iPod?

　　　　　W：It sure is.

　　　　　M：Wow, it's much better than mine.

　　　　　W：It's the latest one.

　　　　　M：I'm jealous.

　　　　　Question：What does the man mean?

　　　　　A. He wishes he had a new iPod.

　　　　　B. He is happy for the woman.

　　　　　C. He wants to borrow the woman's iPod.

　　　* ***iPod*** MP3 的產品之一　　sure〔ʃur〕*adv.* 的確

　　　　wow〔waʊ〕*interj.* 哇（表示驚訝等的叫聲）

　　　　better〔'bɛtɚ〕*adj.* 較好的（good 的比較級）

　　　　mine〔maɪn〕*pron.* 我的（東西）（在此表「我的 MP3」）

　　　　latest〔'letɪst〕*adj.* 最新的

　　　　jealous〔'dʒɛləs〕*adj.* 嫉妒的；羨慕的

　　　　mean〔min〕*v.* 意思是　　wish〔wɪʃ〕*v.* 希望

　　　　borrow〔'bɑro〕*v.* 借（入）

23. (**C**)　W：Are you ready for the geography test?

　　　　　M：Not really.

　　　　　W：How can I help?

　　　　　M：Could you ask me questions about last week's
　　　　　　　lesson?

　　　　　W：No problem.

Question：What will the woman ask the man?

A. When the Ming dynasty ended.

B. What elements water is composed of.

C. The names of the countries of Africa.

* ready（'rɛdɪ）*adj.* 準備好的

  geography（dʒi'ɑgrəfɪ）*n.* 地理

  not really 倒也不見得；也不盡然是

  lesson（'lɛsn̩）*n.* 課程

  No problem. 沒問題。

  dynasty（'daɪnəstɪ）*n.* 朝代

  Ming dynasty 明朝　　end（ɛnd）*v.* 結束

  element（'ɛləmənt）*n.* 元素

  compose（kəm'poz）*v.* 組成

  country（'kʌntrɪ）*n.* 國家

  Africa（'æfrɪkə）*n.* 非洲

24.（ **C** ）W：When is your brother getting married?

M：They haven't decided on a date for the wedding yet.

W：Do you think they will have a long engagement?

M：Probably. My brother is still at university.

Question：What does the boy imply?

A. His brother is not sure whether or not he will get married.

B. His brother's girlfriend is not eager to get married.

C. His brother will get married after he graduates.

* ***get married*** 結婚　　decide〔dɪˈsaɪd〕v. 決定
  date〔det〕n. 日期　　wedding〔ˈwɛdɪŋ〕n. 婚禮
  yet〔jɛt〕adv. 尚（未）（用於否定句）；已經（用於疑問句）
  engagement〔ɪnˈgedʒmənt〕n. 訂婚期間
  probably〔ˈprɑbəblɪ〕adv. 可能
  university〔ˌjunəˈvɝsətɪ〕n. 大學
  imply〔ɪmˈplaɪ〕v. 暗示　　sure〔ʃur〕adj. 確定的
  whether or not~ 是否~　　eager〔ˈigɚ〕adj. 渴望的
  graduate〔ˈgrædʒuˌet〕v. 畢業

25. (**C**)　M：Did you enjoy your studies in Japan?

　　　W：Not really.　I came home early.

　　　M：Why?

　　　W：I got very homesick.

　　Question：Why did the woman leave Japan?

　　A. She finished her studies.

　　B. She couldn't find a suitable place to live.

　　C. She missed her friends and family.

* enjoy〔ɪnˈdʒɔɪ〕v. 喜歡；享受
  studies〔ˈstʌdɪz〕n. pl. 學業
  Japan〔dʒəˈpæn〕n. 日本
  not really 倒也不見得；也不盡然是
  early〔ˈɝlɪ〕adv. 提早　　***get homesick*** 想家
  leave〔liv〕v. 離開　　finish〔ˈfɪnɪʃ〕v. 完成
  suitable〔ˈsutəbl〕adj. 適合的
  place〔ples〕n. 地方；場所　　live〔lɪv〕v. 住
  miss〔mɪs〕v. 想念　　family〔ˈfæməlɪ〕n. 家人

26. (**B**)　W : Do you know the names of all the planets?

　　　　M : Yes, that's sure to be on the test.

　　　　W : What else should we study?

　　　　M : We should know how scientists think the universe
　　　　　　　was formed.

　　　　Question : What class are they discussing?

　　　　A. Geography.　　　B. Science.　　　C. University.

　　　*　planet ('plænɪt) n. 行星　　　else (ɛls) adj. 別的；其他的
　　　　　scientist ('saɪəntɪst) n. 科學家
　　　　　universe ('junə,vɝs) n. 宇宙　　　form (fɔrm) v. 形成
　　　　　discuss (dɪ'skʌs) v. 討論
　　　　　geography (dʒi'ɑgrəfɪ) n. 地理
　　　　　science ('saɪəns) n. 科學
　　　　　university (,junə'vɝsətɪ) n. 大學

27. (**B**)　M : Isn't that your dog barking outside?

　　　　W : Yes, but just ignore him.

　　　　M : Maybe he needs something.

　　　　W : No, he just wants attention.

　　　　Question : What does the woman ask the man to do?

　　　　A. Pay attention to her dog.

　　　　B. Pay no attention to the barking dog.

　　　　C. Find out why the dog is barking.

　　　*　bark (bɑrk) v. 吠叫　　　outside ('aut'saɪd) adv. 在外面
　　　　　just (dʒʌst) adv. 請 (委婉的祈使語氣)；只是
　　　　　ignore (ɪg'nor) v. 忽視；不理睬
　　　　　maybe ('mebi) adv. 可能；或許
　　　　　attention (ə'tɛnʃən) n. 注意　　　ask (æsk) v. 要求
　　　　　pay attention to 注意　　　***find out*** 查出

28. (**B**) W: Do you have any change?

M: Yes. How much do you need?

W: Twenty dollars.

M: Here's forty. Why don't you get me a drink, too?

Question: What does the woman ask the man to do?

A. Get her a drink.

B. Give her some coins.

C. Change his order.

* change〔tʃendʒ〕n. 零錢　v. 改變
Why don't you～? 你為何不～？（表提議）
get〔gɛt〕v. 買　　drink〔drɪŋk〕n. 飲料
give〔gɪv〕v. 給　　coin〔kɔɪn〕n. 硬幣
order〔'ɔrdɚ〕n. 點的菜

29. (**B**) W: What a beautiful plant.

M: Thank you. I grew it from a seed.

W: Really? How long did it take?

M: A few months.

Question: Which of the following is true?

A. The man bought the plant a few months ago.

B. The man planted the plant himself.

C. The woman does not know how many seeds to plant.

* plant〔plænt〕n. 植物　v. 種植　　grow〔gro〕v. 種植
seed〔sid〕n. 種子　　**How long～?** ～多久？
take〔tek〕v. 花費（時間）　　**a few** 幾個
month〔mʌnθ〕n. 月　　**the following** 下列（事物）
true〔tru〕adj. 正確的　　ago〔ə'go〕adv. …以前

30. (**A**) M: Were you absent yesterday?

W: Yes, I had a cold. Did I miss anything important?

M: Well, we're going to have a test today in English class.

W: Oh, no. That's terrible news.

Question: How does the woman feel?

A. Worried.　　　　B. Cold.

C. Calm.

* absent ('æbsṇt) adj. 缺席的　　**have a cold** 感冒
miss (mɪs) v. 錯過
important (ɪm'pɔrtṇt) adj. 重要的
test (tɛst) n. 考試　　class (klæs) n. 課
terrible ('tɛrəbḷ) adj. 可怕的　　news (njuz) n. 消息
feel (fil) v. 覺得　　worried ('wɝɪd) adj. 擔心的
cold (kold) adj. 冷的　　calm (kɑm) adj. 冷靜的

二、閱讀能力測驗

第一部份：詞彙和結構

1. (**C**) Nara forgot <u>to eat</u> her dinner, so she ate at 11 p.m.

娜拉忘記<u>去吃</u>晚餐，所以她在晚上十一點吃。

$\begin{cases} \text{forget} + \text{V-ing} & \text{忘記已做~（動作已做）} \\ \text{forget} + \text{to V.} & \text{忘記去做~（動作未做）} \end{cases}$

依句意「她在晚上十一點吃」，表示她忘了吃，故選 (C)
to eat。

* forget (fɚ'gɛt) v. 忘記
p.m. ('pi'ɛm) adv. 下午；午後 (= *P.M.*)

2. (**A**) I'll <u>leave</u> a light on for you if you come home late.

你如果晚回家，我會留個燈給你。

「leave＋受詞（a light）＋受詞補語（on）」作「使…處於某種狀態」解，故依句意，應選 (A)。

* light〔laɪt〕n. 燈　　on〔ɑn〕adv.（電器）開著
late〔let〕adv. 晚

3. (**B**) It was raining, so my mother didn't allow me to swim <u>in</u> the river.

當時正在下雨，所以我母親不准我<u>在</u>河<u>裡</u>游泳。

(A) on〔ɑn〕prep. 在…上面

(B) *in*〔ɪn〕prep. 在…裡面

(C) by〔baɪ〕prep. 在…旁邊

(D) at〔æt〕prep. 在…（地點）

游泳應是在河裡，故應選 (B)。

* rain〔ren〕v. 下雨　　allow〔ə'laʊ〕v. 允許
swim〔swɪm〕v. 游泳　　river〔'rɪvɚ〕n. 河

4. (**A**) The little girl who is walking a dog is my <u>niece</u>.

那個正在遛狗的小女孩是我<u>姪女</u>。

(A) *niece*〔nis〕n. 姪女；外甥女

(B) nephew〔'nɛfju〕n. 姪兒；外甥

(C) aunt〔ænt〕n. 阿姨

(D) female〔'fimel〕n. 女性

* walk〔wɔlk〕v. 遛（狗）

5. (**A**) My teacher <u>indicated</u> many spelling mistakes in my English composition.
我的老師在我的英文作文裡，<u>指出</u>很多拼字的錯誤。

    (A) ***indicate*** (ˈɪndə͵ket) *v.* 指出

    (B) inspire (ɪnˈspaɪr) *v.* 激勵；給予靈感

    (C) interrupt (͵ɪntəˈrʌpt) *v.* 打斷

    (D) invent (ɪnˈvɛnt) *v.* 發明

  * spelling (ˈspɛlɪŋ) *n.* 拼字　　mistake (məˈstek) *n.* 錯誤
composition (͵kɑmpəˈzɪʃən) *n.* 作文

6. (**B**) I am just an <u>ordinary</u> person.　I just want a regular life.
我只是個<u>平凡</u>人。我只想過普通的生活。

    (A) evil (ˈivl̩) *adj.* 邪惡的

    (B) ***ordinary*** (ˈɔrdn͵ɛrɪ) *adj.* 普通的；平凡的

    (C) excellent (ˈɛksl̩ənt) *adj.* 優秀的

    (D) intelligent (ɪnˈtɛləgənt) *adj.* 聰明的

  * regular (ˈrɛgjələ) *adj.* 普通的；一般的
life (laɪf) *n.* 生活

7. (**D**) Jason : My secretary didn't <u>attend</u> yesterday's meeting.
Jane　: You mean she was absent from the meeting.
傑森：我的秘書沒有<u>參加</u>昨天的會議。
珍　：你是指那個會議她缺席了。

    (A) enter (ˈɛntə) *v.* 進入

    (B) prepare (prɪˈpɛr) *v.* 準備

    (C) report (rɪˈport) *v.* 報告

    (D) ***attend*** (əˈtɛnd) *v.* 參加

  * secretary (ˈsɛkrə͵tɛrɪ) *n.* 秘書　　meeting (ˈmitɪŋ) *n.* 會議
mean (min) *v.* 意思是　　absent (ˈæbsn̩t) *adj.* 缺席的

8. (**C**) J.K. Rowling is one of the <u>most famous</u> writers in the world.

J.K.羅琳是世界上<u>最知名</u>的作家之一。

由句尾的 in the world 可知，其比較的對象有三者以上，故應選 (C)，famous 的最高級。

* ***J.K. Rowling*** J.K.羅琳 (《哈利波特》的作者)
famous〔'feməs〕*adj.* 有名的　　writer〔'raɪtɚ〕*n.* 作家

9. (**D**) Mary is not smart <u>but</u> diligent.

瑪麗不聰明，<u>但是</u>很勤奮。

這題依句意應選 (D) ***but***，形成 not A but B「不是 A 而是 B」的句型。smart 和 diligent 都是形容詞，應選連接詞，故 (A)不合。句中並沒有比較級的形容詞，故 (B)不合。(C) as 作「如…一般」解，在此不合。

* smart〔smɑrt〕*adj.* 聰明的
diligent〔'dɪlədʒənt〕*adj.* 勤勉的

10. (**B**) <u>Seldom</u> do I stay at home during holidays.

假日時我<u>很少</u>待在家。

主詞與動詞倒裝，但句尾不是問號，故應選 (B) ***Seldom***。表否定意味的副詞放在句首時，句子須倒裝。

* seldom〔'sɛldəm〕*adv.* 很少
stay〔ste〕*v.* 停留
holiday〔'hɑlə,de〕*n.* 假日

11. (**D**) Jason : Didn't you take the garbage out yet?

Jane : <u>No, I didn't</u>. The garbage truck hasn't come yet.

傑森：妳還沒把垃圾拿出去嗎？

珍 ：<u>是的，我沒有拿</u>。垃圾車還沒來。

不帶疑問詞的疑問句，通常用 yes 或 no 回答。且若回答 yes，則其後的句子應爲肯定；若回答 no，則其後的句子應爲否定，即使是否定的疑問句，也要遵守上述的原則，故選 (D)。

* ***take out*** 拿出去 garbage〔'gɑrbɪdʒ〕n. 垃圾

yet〔jɛt〕adv. 尚（未）（用於否定句）

truck〔trʌk〕n. 卡車 ***garbage truck*** 垃圾車

12. (**B**) I am used to <u>brushing</u> my teeth before going to bed.

我習慣在上床睡覺前<u>刷</u>牙。

be used to「習慣～」中的 to 是介系詞，故其後應接名詞或動名詞，故選(B)。

* brush〔brʌʃ〕v. 刷

tooth〔tuθ〕n. 牙齒（複數形爲 teeth〔tiθ〕）

go to bed 上床睡覺

13. (**C**) Dinah has lived in Iland <u>since</u> 1981.

黛娜<u>從</u> 1981 年就已經住在宜蘭了。

現在完成式可表「過去持續到現在的動作或狀態」，所以黛娜現在仍住在宜蘭，故 (A) before 和 (B) in 不合。

現在完成式常與 since 和 for 連用，當它們都作介系詞時，其差異爲：

since + 特定時間點 自…以來

for + 時間長度 在…期間一直

故應選 (C)。 * ***Iland*** 宜蘭

14. (**C**)　The baby was made <u>to cry</u> by the big noise.

那很大的噪音使小嬰兒哭了。

使役動詞的主動與被動，其差異如下：

$\begin{cases} \text{A make + B + V.} \quad \text{A 使 B}\sim \\ \text{= B + be made + to V. + by A} \end{cases}$

這題是被動，故應選 (C)。

* noise〔nɔɪz〕*n.* 噪音

15. (**B**)　It's <u>such</u> a nice day that many people are going on a picnic.　今天天氣<u>這麼</u>好，所以很多人去野餐。

空格後是一名詞片語（ a nice day ），故應選形容詞 (B) *such* 來修飾。

* *such…that*～　如此…所以～　　*go on a picnic* 去野餐

第二部份：段落填空

Questions 16-21

　　Last Friday I got really wet from head to <u>toe</u>. After

16

<u>finishing</u> work, I left <u>for</u> home on my old bicycle. I was going

17　　　　　　18

fast because it was <u>about</u> to rain. After five minutes, my bike

19

broke down <u>with</u> a strange noise. Just then, it started to rain.

20

I walked my bike home quickly in the rain. I didn't complain

because I didn't get hurt. <u>Actually</u>, it felt kind of refreshing to

21

feel the water washing down on me.

上星期五，我從頭到腳濕透了。工作完之後，我騎我的老腳踏車回家。因為快下雨了，所以我騎得很快。五分鐘之後，我的腳踏車在發出怪聲的同時，壞掉了。就在當時，開始下雨了。在雨中，我快速地推著我的腳踏車走回家。我並沒有抱怨，因為我沒受傷。事實上，水沖洗著我，讓我感覺有些神清氣爽。

get〔gɛt〕v. 成為…狀態　　really〔ˈrɪəlɪ〕adv. 實在
wet〔wɛt〕adj. 濕的　　fast〔fæst〕adv. 迅速地
break down 發生故障　　strange〔strendʒ〕adj. 奇怪的
noise〔nɔɪz〕n. 雜音；噪音　　**just then** 正當那時
start〔stɑrt〕v. 開始　　walk〔wɔk〕v. 把（自行車）推著走
home〔hom〕adv. 往家
complain〔kəmˈplen〕v. 抱怨　　**get hurt** 受傷
feel〔fil〕v. 使人覺得　　**kind of** 有一點
refreshing〔rɪˈfrɛʃɪŋ〕adj. 令人爽快的　　**wash down** 沖洗

16. (**D**)　(A) ankle〔ˈæŋkḷ〕n. 腳踝
　　　　(B) wrist〔rɪst〕n. 手腕
　　　　(C) elbow〔ˈɛl͵bo〕n. 手肘
　　　　(D) **toe**〔to〕n. 腳趾　　**from head to toe** 從頭到腳

17. (**C**)　after 可當連接詞或介系詞，由選項中均無主詞可知，after 在這裡當介系詞，介系詞後只能接名詞或動名詞，故應選 (C) **finishing**。　　* finish〔ˈfɪnɪʃ〕v. 完成

18. (**B**)　主角工作完成，要回家了，故應選 (B) **for** 形成 **leave for**「動身前往」。

19. (**B**)　天空不會「被」下雨，所以若選 (A)(C)會形成被動態，不合句意。(D) almost 可直接修飾動詞，動詞前不可加 to，故 (D) 用法不合。故選 (B) **about** 形成 **be about to**「即將」。

20. (**C**) 按照句意，應選 (C) *with*「與…同時」。

21. (**A**) (A) *actually*（'æktʃʊəlɪ）*adv.* 事實上
　　　　 (B) usually（'juʒʊəlɪ）*adv.* 通常
　　　　 (C) finally（'faɪnlɪ）*adv.* 最後；終於
　　　　 (D) probably（'prɑbəblɪ）*adv.* 可能

Questions 22-25

The second <u>term</u> started today.　It was very hard <u>for</u> me to
　　　　　 22　　　　　　　　　　　　　　　　　　　　　 23
get up at six-thirty this morning.　But it was nice to see my

classmates again after one month.　The first class was math.

I'm not good <u>at</u> math, so I felt the period was very long.
　　　　　　 24
After school, my tennis club had a meeting.　After the meeting,

we spent an hour <u>playing</u> tennis.
　　　　　　　　 25

　　第二學期今天開始。今天早上六點半起床，對我來說非常困難。但
是很高興在一個月之後，再次看到我的同學們。第一堂課是數學。我的
數學不好，所以我覺得這堂課好長。放學之後，我的網球社有個會議。
會議之後，我打了一個小時的網球。

　　　second（'sɛkənd）*adj.* 第二的　　 start（stɑrt）*v.* 開始
　　　hard（hɑrd）*adj.* 困難的　　 ***get up*** 起床
　　　nice（naɪs）*adj.* 愉快的；高興的
　　　math（mæθ）*n.* 數學（= *mathematics*）
　　　period（'pɪrɪəd）*n.* 期間　　 long（lɔŋ）*adj.* 長的；久的
　　　tennis（'tɛnɪs）*n.* 網球　　 club（klʌb）*n.* 社團
　　　meeting（'mitɪŋ）*n.* 會議
　　　spend（spɛnd）*v.* 花（時間）

22. (**C**)　(A) class〔klæs〕*n.* 課程
　　　　　(B) exam〔ɪgˋzæm〕*n.* 考試
　　　　　　(= *examination*〔ɪg͵zæməˋneʃən〕)
　　　　　(C) *term*〔tɜm〕*n.* 學期　　　(D) season〔ˋsizn̩〕*n.* 季節

23. (**A**)　這是一個句型：主詞＋be 動詞＋形容詞＋for＋受詞，作
　　　　　「某事對某人而言是～」解，故選 (A)。

24. (**B**)　*be good at* 擅長於

25. (**C**)　「花時間做某事」的句型為：spend＋時間＋(in) +V-ing，
　　　　　故應選 (C) *playing*。　　　* *play tennis* 打網球

第三部份：閱讀理解

Question 26

```
┌─────────────────────────┐
│                         │
│         徵　人           │
│                         │
│        全　　職          │
│      一週工作五天        │
│    有經驗的麵包師父      │
│                         │
│         ＊＊＊           │
│                         │
│      史都華麵包店        │
│                         │
└─────────────────────────┘
```

　　wanted〔ˋwɑntɪd〕*adj.* 徵求…的
　　full-time〔ˋfulˋtaɪm〕*adj.* 全職的
　　experienced〔ɪkˋspɪrɪənst〕*adj.* 經驗豐富的
　　baker〔ˋbekɚ〕*n.* 麵包師父
　　Stewart〔ˋstjuɚt〕*n.* 史都華（男子名）
　　bakery〔ˋbekərɪ〕*n.* 麵包店

26. (**D**) 史都華麵包店需要哪一種人？

(A) 全職賣麵包的人。

(B) 會經營麵包店的員工。

(C) 有經驗的廚師。

(D) <u>做烘焙工作很多年的人。</u>

* kind〔kaɪnd〕*n.* 種類　　need〔nid〕*v.* 需要
sell〔sɛl〕*v.* 賣；銷售　　bread〔brɛd〕*n.* 麵包
employee〔͵ɛmplɔɪ'i〕*n.* 員工
manage〔'mænɪdʒ〕*v.* 經營；管理　　bake〔bek〕*v.* 烘焙

Questions 27-29

　　下面的圖表顯示向五個國家的父母調查的結果，題目是：為什麼孩子對他們很重要。他們被要求從七個選項中，選出最重要的三個主要原因。例如：對日本父母而言，最重要的三個原因是：第四項—強化家族關係（百分之五十一）、第五項—藉由養育孩子來自我提升（百分之六十）、第七項—養育有責任感的公民（百分之四十五）。

項目	日本	韓國	美國	英國	法國
①看到自己能在未來的世代繼續存在	35%	31%	32%	17%	59%
②傳宗接代	24%	68%	28%	17%	26%
③養兒防老	10%	38%	8%	7%	8%
④強化家族關係	51%	25%	50%	55%	66%
⑤藉由養育孩子來自我提升	60%	19%	54%	69%	35%
⑥喜歡養育孩子	20%	19%	50%	71%	39%
⑦養育有責任感的公民	45%	40%	46%	28%	15%

following〔'faləwɪŋ〕adj. 下列的

chart〔tʃart〕n. 圖表　　show〔ʃo〕v. 顯示

result〔rɪ'zʌlt〕n. 結果　　survey〔sə've〕n. 調查

country〔'kʌntrɪ〕n. 國家　　choose〔tʃuz〕v. 選擇

main〔men〕adj. 主要的　　reason〔'rizn〕n. 理由

for example 例如　　Japanese〔,dʒæpə'niz〕adj. 日本的

item〔'aɪtəm〕n. 項目　　strengthen〔'strɛŋθən〕v. 加強

ties〔taɪz〕n. 關係；情分　　*family ties* 家族關係

develop〔dɪ'vɛləp〕v. 發展

through〔θru〕prep. 透過；經由　　raise〔rez〕v. 養育

responsible〔rɪ'spɑnsəbḷ〕adj. 有責任的

citizen〔'sɪtəzn̩〕n. 公民　　Japan〔dʒə'pæn〕n. 日本

Korea〔kə'riə〕n. 韓國

U.S.A. 美國（= *United States of America*）

Britain〔'brɪtən〕n. 英國　　France〔fræns〕n. 法國

continue on 繼續存在　　future〔'fjutʃə〕adj. 未來的

generation〔,dʒɛnə'reʃən〕n. 世代

keep〔kip〕v. 保存　　line〔laɪn〕n. 血統

receive〔rɪ'siv〕v. 接受　　care〔kɛr〕n. 照顧

old age 老年　　enjoy〔ɪn'dʒɔɪ〕v. 喜歡；享受

27. (**D**) 在所有的國家中，只有_____父母認為，傳宗接代是養育
孩子最重要的理由。

(A) American〔ə'mɛrɪkən〕adj. 美國的

(B) French〔frɛntʃ〕adj. 法國的

(C) Japanese〔,dʒæpə'niz〕adj. 日本的

(D) *Korean*〔kə'riən〕adj. 韓國的

* among〔ə'mʌŋ〕prep. 在…之間

think〔θɪŋk〕v. 認為

28. (**B**) 大部分的國家認為，哪一個項目是他們養育孩子主要的理由
之一？

(A) 項目一。   (B) 項目四。
(C) 項目五。   (D) 項目六。

* most〔most〕*adj.* 大多數的

29. (**B**) 哪兩個國家養育小孩有相同的主要理由？

(A) 日本和韓國。   (B) 美國和英國。
(C) 英國和法國。   (D) 日本和美國。

Questions 30-32

四月				
蘋果中學				
星期一	星期二	星期三	星期四	星期五
1/ 學校會議	2/ 籃球小組會議	3/ 藝術展 ⟶	4/ ⟶	5/ 野餐
8/ 電腦小組會議	9/ 實地調查旅行	10/ 歌唱小組會議	11/ 英文小組會議	12/ 棒球小組會議
15/ 學校會議	16/ 半天： 中午放學	17/ 電影欣賞： 變臉	18/ 科學小組會議	19/ 才藝表演
22/ 考試 ⟶	23/	24/	25/	26/ ⟶
29/ 畢業會議				

April〔'eprəl〕n. 四月　　middle〔'mɪdḷ〕adj. 中等的

middle school 中學　　meeting〔'mitɪŋ〕n. 會議

basketball〔'bæskɪt,bɔl〕n. 籃球

group〔grup〕n. 團體　　art〔ɑrt〕adj. 藝術的

show〔ʃo〕n. 展示　　field〔fild〕n. 田野

trip〔trɪp〕n. 旅行　　***field trip*** 野外實地調查旅行

baseball〔'bes'bɔl〕n. 棒球

half〔hæf〕adj. 一半的　　leave〔liv〕v. 離開

noon〔nun〕n. 正午　　film〔fɪlm〕n. 電影

Face Off 電影名（台灣譯為《變臉》）

science〔'saɪəns〕n. 科學　　talent〔'tælənt〕n. 才能

exam〔ɪg'zæm〕n. 考試（= *examination*〔ɪg,zæmə'neʃən〕）

graduation〔,grædʒʊ'eʃən〕n. 畢業

30. (**C**)　學生們在四月有＿＿＿＿學校會議。

　　(A) 六次　　　　　　　(B) 三次

　　(C) 二次　　　　　　　(D) 一次

　　* time〔taɪm〕n. 次數

　　　twice〔twaɪs〕adv. 兩次

　　　once〔wʌns〕adv. 一次

31. (**A**)　由上面的圖表我們可以看出，這個學校有兩個＿＿＿＿團體。

　　(A) ***sports***〔sports〕adj. 運動的

　　(B) art〔ɑrt〕adj. 藝術的

　　(C) science〔'saɪəns〕n. 科學

　　(D) language〔'læŋgwɪdʒ〕n. 語言

　　* above〔ə'bʌv〕adj. 上面的

　　　chart〔tʃɑrt〕n. 圖表

32. (**B**) 藝術展持續多久？

    (A) 一天。   (B) 二天。

    (C) 三天。   (D) 四天。

    * *How long~?* ～多久？   last〔læst〕v. 持續

Questions 33-35

    Mozart was born in 1756. Everyone knows he was one of the world's most famous music composers. Mozart had an amazing early life. He was writing excellent music by the age of five. At the age of six, he was playing for kings and queens all over Europe. His talent and genius made him very famous.

    莫札特生於 1756 年。大家都知道他是世界上最知名的作曲家之一。莫札特有個令人驚訝的早年生活，當他五歲時，就寫了很棒的音樂。六歲時，他向全歐洲的國王和皇后演奏。他的才能和天份使他非常有名。

Mozart〔'mozɑrt〕n. 莫札特   ***be born*** 出生

famous〔'feməs〕adj. 有名的

composer〔kəm'pozɚ〕n. 作曲家

amazing〔ə'mezɪŋ〕adj. 驚人的

early〔'ɝlɪ〕adj. 初期的   life〔laɪf〕n. 生活

excellent〔'ɛkslənt〕adj. 極好的

play〔ple〕v. 演奏   ***all over*** 遍及

Europe〔'jurəp〕n. 歐洲

talent〔'tælənt〕n. 才能

genius〔'dʒinjəs〕n. 天才

make〔mek〕v. 使…變得～

However, Mozart's adult life was a difficult one. He never really found a steady (穩定的) job that could last for more than a year. He was too impatient to teach and most jobs creating music were only part-time. Therefore, Mozart was always struggling to find work. He often spent too much money so that he often had to borrow money.

然而,莫札特的成年生活卻很艱難。他從沒找到一個真正可以持續一年以上的穩定工作。他太沒耐心了,以致於不能教書,而且大部分創作音樂的工作,都只是兼差性質的。因此,莫札特老是很掙扎地在找工作。他常常花太多錢,以致於常常需要借錢。

however〔haʊˈɛvə〕adv. 然而
adult〔əˈdʌlt〕adj. 成年的
difficult〔ˈdɪfəˌkʌlt〕adj. 困難的
really〔ˈrɪəlɪ〕adv. 真正地
steady〔ˈstɛdɪ〕adj. 穩定的　　job〔dʒɑb〕n. 工作
last〔læst〕v. 持續　　*too…to~* 太…以致於不能~
impatient〔ɪmˈpeʃənt〕adj. 沒耐心的
create〔krɪˈet〕v. 創造
part-time〔ˈpɑrtˈtaɪm〕adj. 兼差的
therefore〔ˈðɛrˌfor〕adv. 因此
struggle〔ˈstrʌgl̩〕v. 掙扎
spend〔spɛnd〕v. 花（錢）
so that 所以;以便於
borrow〔ˈbɑro〕v. 借（入）

It's a pity that Mozart died from a high fever and brief illness at the young age of 35. It is even sadder because he died poor and almost all alone.

遺憾的是，莫札特在三十五歲就死於高燒和短暫的疾病。甚至更令人悲傷的是，因為他死的時候很窮，而且幾乎是孤單一人。

pity〔'pɪtɪ〕n. 遺憾的事	**die from…** 因…而死
fever〔'fivɚ〕n. 發燒	brief〔brif〕adj. 短暫的
illness〔'ɪlnɪs〕n. 疾病	even〔'ivən〕adv. 甚至
sad〔sæd〕adj. 悲傷的	poor〔pur〕adj. 窮的
die poor 死的時候很窮	alone〔ə'lon〕adj. 孤獨的
all alone 孤單地	

33. (**C**) 莫札特做了什麼驚人的事？
   (A) 他只活了三十五年。
   (B) 他背誦了許多名字和號碼。
   (C) 他在許多國家表演。
   (D) 他教國王和皇后音樂。

   * memorize〔'mɛmə,raɪz〕v. 背誦
     perform〔pɚ'fɔrm〕v. 表演

34. (**D**) 莫札特的一生，有_____的困擾。
   (A) 和家人相處
   (B) 找學生來教
   (C) 聽力
   (D) 賺錢和存錢

 * during (ˋdjʊrɪŋ) *prep.* 在…期間

 have trouble with… 有…的麻煩（困擾）

 have trouble (*in*) ***V-ing***… 很難～

 pupil (ˋpjupl̩) *n.* 學生　　hearing (ˋhɪrɪŋ) *n.* 聽力

 make money 賺錢　　save (sev) *v.* 儲存

35.(**B**)　莫札特最後發生什麼事？

(A)　他染上熱病，因而變聾。

(B)　一場病造成他的英年早逝。

(C)　他死於寂寞。

(D)　他在一場意外中喪生。

 * finally (ˋfaɪnl̩ɪ) *adv.* 最後

 ～happen to… ～發生在…

 catch (kætʃ) *v.* 染上（病）

 fever (ˋfivɚ) *n.* 熱病；發燒

 deaf (dɛf) *adj.* 聾的

 cause (kɔz) *v.* 造成

 early (ˋɝlɪ) *adj.* （比預期）早的

 death (dɛθ) *n.* 死亡

 die of… 因…而死

 loneliness (ˋlonlɪnɪs) *n.* 寂寞

 be killed （因意外而）死亡

 accident (ˋæksədənt) *n.* 意外

Elemetary Level

劉毅英文「初級英檢保證班」

現在孩子學英文愈來愈早,很多國小生就已經具備了考「初級英檢」的能力,但礙於法令無法在國小時考試,所以國小就開始準備「初級英檢」,國一就要通過「初級英檢」,才高人一等。

I. 收費標準:*19,900元*(贈送代辦報名費初試和複試各一次,價值*1,080*元,本班幫同學代辦報名)

【全年循環上課,隨到隨上,考試當週停課一次。過年、主要學校月期考,停課一次。】

※一次繳費,直到考取認證為止!

II. 上課方式:完全比照97年最新「初檢」命題標準命題,我們將新編的試題,印成一整本,讓同學閱讀複習方便。老師視情況上課,讓同學做測驗,同學不需要交卷,老師立刻講解,一次一次地訓練,讓同學輕鬆取得認證。

III. 保證辦法:同學只要報一次名,就可以終生上課,考上為止,但必須每年至少考一次「初級英檢」,憑成績單才可以繼續上課,否則就必須重新報名,才能再上課。報名參加「初級英檢測驗」,但缺考,則視同沒有報名。

IV. 報名贈書:1.初級英檢公佈字彙
2.初級英語寫作能力測驗(價值280元)
3.初級英檢模擬試題(價值720元)
4.初級英檢聽力測驗(書＋CD一套)
(價值680元)

V. 上課教材:

※本班獨家教材,
市面不售,非賣品。

VI. 報名地點:台北市許昌街17號6樓(壽德大樓)TEL:(02)2389-5212

初級英檢模擬試題④

主　　　編/劉　毅
發 行 所/學習出版有限公司　　　☎(02) 2704-5525
郵 撥 帳 號/0512727-2 學習出版社帳戶
登 記 證/局版台業 2179 號
印 刷 所/裕強彩色印刷有限公司
台 北 門 市/台北市許昌街 10 號 2 F　☎(02) 2331-4060・2331-9209
台灣總經銷/紅螞蟻圖書有限公司　　☎(02) 2795-3656
美國總經銷/ Evergreen Book Store　☎(818) 2813622
本公司網址　www.learnbook.com.tw
電 子 郵 件　learnbook@learnbook.com.tw

書＋MP3 一片售價：新台幣二百八十元正

2008 年 10 月 1 日新修訂

ISBN 978-986-231-000-7